Murder in Times Square

MURDER IN TIMES SQUARE

A DEIDRE MYSTERY

A Novel

BY

William Baer

MANY WORDS PRESS
An imprint of Able Muse Press

Many Words Press

www.manywords.com

Library of Congress Cataloging-in-Publication Data

Names: Baer, William, 1948- author.
Title: Murder in Times Square : a novel / by William Baer.
Description: San Jose, CA : Many Words Press, 2022. | Series: A Deirdre mystery; book 1
Identifiers: LCCN 2021036232 (print) | LCCN 2021036233 (ebook) | ISBN 9781773491011 (paperback) | ISBN 9781773491028 (ebook)
Subjects: GSAFD: Mystery fiction.
Classification: LCC PS3552.A3324 M87 2022 (print) | LCC PS3552.A3324 (ebook) | DDC 813/.54--dc23
LC record available at https://lccn.loc.gov/2021036232
LC ebook record available at https://lccn.loc.gov/2021036233

Printed in the United States of America

Cover image: *Times Lens* by Alexander Pepple
(with *Bright Lights of Times Square* by Justin Brown and *Red Garment* by Jr Korpa)

Cover & book design by Alexander Pepple

Many Words Press is an imprint of Able Muse Press—at www.ablemusepress.com

Many Words Press
467 Saratoga Avenue #602
San Jose, CA 95129

For my family and friends—

especially my aunt, Evelyn Stuart,
who designed sweaters for Halston,
Adolfo, Bill Blass, and others

CONTENTS

Murder in Times Square

Beauty is not caused.

It is.

— Emily Dickinson

Murder in Times Square

1. Times Square One

I WAS SITTING on a block of ice freezing my ass off.

Actually, that was a bit earlier.

(I'll get back to it later.)

In the meantime, a few blocks away, a pretty young girl in a red dress was standing on a rooftop, staring down at the greatest city in the world, thinking about what?

Her past, her problems, something she needed to do?

Was she alone?

Was she waiting for someone?

Was she waiting for something?

A lover, a message, the nerve to jump?

Later, when I was cutting through Times Square, focused on M&Ms, I heard someone scream. A tourist from Switzerland. For some reason, I looked up. Into the night. Then I saw her. Actually, I saw her ruby red designer dress as she flew off the roof of Times Square One, falling twenty-five stories to the center of the universe.

What Manhattanites modestly call the Great White Way.

The Tenderloin.

The Crossroads of the World.

The blood was slowly pooling around the poor girl's head.

Carlos was right behind me.

"It's not for you," he said, meaning that I never get involved with suicides.

Just homicides.

"Come on, Deirdre, let's get out of here."

He was still a bit edgy about the telegram I'd received earlier.

I shrugged.

"Let's see what happens."

It was Times Square on a Friday night in the middle of June. The huge square from Forty-Second to Forty-Seventh was jammed with out-of-towners, foreign tourists, and hectic New Yorkers all moving rather peacefully, in varying directions, beneath the flashing, wildly colored, ever-moving lights of the neons, LEDs, and jumbotrons.

From Duffy Square in the north to Times Square One in the south, the crowds hustled here and there, within blaring overlapping musics, within brilliantly colored lights, heading for the Hard Rock Café, Madame Tussauds, Planet Hollywood, or Ripley's Odditorium.

Or, like me, M&M's World.

Fortunately, at the south end of the square, the crowd was a bit more relaxed and dispersed, milling around in front of Times Square One, also known as the old Times Building, which, when it was first built in 1905, was the second tallest building in the world. These days, it was one of the most visited, stared-at, and filmed buildings on the entire planet, given its famous signs, given the universally known fact that it dropped the glittering New Year's Eve ball on the last day of December every year.

Every year since 1907.

Of course, like so much else that's beautiful in this world, its beauty was only skin-deep. Times Square One is actually, amazingly, just an empty shell, a glitzy exterior wrapped around a lifeless interior. Except for a handful of retail stores on the first few floors, the entire building is empty, all the way up to the twenty-fifth floor. But beauty, as it often reminds us, typically finds a way to pay for itself, and the advertising revenue from the building's twenty-six signs, generally considered the most valuable signs in the world, generate well over four million dollars each year.

Who needs tenants?

A few minutes ago, the tourists on the street below were taking turns craning their necks to look upward, past the famous "zipper" news crawl, past the jumbotron, past the tremendous Budweiser sign, past the huge Toshiba sign, to stare at the dark roof of the building, maybe seeing the flagpole, maybe trying to imagine the New Year's Eve ball coming down even though it was more than six months away.

Then lovely Swiss Miss looked up and screamed.

As a sudden flash of red seemed to hurl itself off the rooftop, as if slow motion, as if surreal, as if a dream, dropping like a stone in front of the multicolored signs, thudding to the street at West Forty-Third.

Hitting no one, just the pavement.

Immediately, one of the cops from Midtown South, a new guy I didn't know too well, rushed over and started moving the crowd away. At the same time, I managed to wiggle through the ever-tightening crowd of onlookers to look at the dead body lying in front of me. She was remarkably beautiful, very young, dressed in an elegantly red Donna Karan evening gown.

Which I recognized.

(The dress, not the girl.)

Within an ever-expanding pool of dark blood.

2. Cover Shoot

AN HOUR EARLIER, I was sitting on a block of ice wearing a pure-white Ralph Lauren, a lovely crew-neck sweater with a tiny, over-the-heart, red maple leaf. Tonight's shoot was scheduled for the winter cover and its accompanying editorial spread in *Elle*, one of my favorite magazines. We'd already been at it for about three hours, changing the blocks of ice every twenty minutes, with the boys providing new, dry, and heated sitting pads to keep my bottom from freezing solid. Nevertheless, I managed to keep my smile warm and sunny, moving through my poses ever so slowly and comfortably as Eduardo's Hasselblad H4D clicked off countless exposures.

"Perfect, dear!" Eduardo would say as he continued working, intense as ever, perfectly pleased.

"Keep smiling, Deirdre!"

I've always enjoyed working with Eduardo, who's focused yet friendly, with a pleasant sense of humor. Over the years, I've been fortunate to work with more than fifty of the "name" photographers in the business, and I've definitely got my favorites, but Eduardo is always number one. Back when I was twelve years old and scared to death, Eduardo did my very first testing, and even today, both my portfolio and my composite card have a shot or two or three from Eduardo. Usually a headshot. He'd also done some of my more "famous" shoots: the "walk on water" in the Valentino evening gown, those funny but creepy ads with a real (!) skeleton for Nature's Bounty, the popular "suspended in the mist" ads for London Fog, and those cutesy but attention-grabbing ads for Band-Aid.

Last year, I made over $3.2 million, and although I know it sounds ridiculous, even though it kept me in the "top ten," I needed every single penny. But I never minded the work, and I remain devotedly grateful to my mentor Rexana and my agent Sabrina, not to mention Sabrina's exclusive client list because *that's* where the money is. These days, she's made me the primary face for both Lacoste and Tommy Hilfiger. Not to mention high-visibility deals with Lauren, Olay, Apple (their "hip" iPod ads), General Motors (Corvette convertible), Coke, Major League Baseball, and Tiffany. I was also especially proud of two of my less lucrative deals: the one with Mars Inc. for M&Ms, where I gladly shared the spotlight with various "spokescandies" like wiseguy "Red" and lovable "Yellow," and a much different deal with Everlast Inc. from the Bronx, the world's premier manufacturers of professional boxing equipment, where I'd actually got to do some ads with big-time champs like Manny Pacquiao, Bernard Hopkins, and Triple G.

I was also lucky in other ways. For starters, my "look" was remarkably versatile. I was just as comfortable in a Dior evening gown as I was portraying the smiling girl-next-door with a green Band-Aid on my cheek for Johnson & Johnson. Thanks to Sabrina, I'd also become "mononymous," a "one-namer," in a business that values individuality, and I'd definitely become my own brand, although I'd never compare myself to the legendary one-namers like Giselle, Iman, Veruschka, or Twiggy.

"Twiggy was the best," my uncle said one time, with all the authority of a New York Police Captain. "Case closed."

"Yeah, you're right for a change," my old man agreed, which he seldom did, with all the authority of a man who'd battled in the boxing ring for over fifteen years.

They were both right.

Rexana, who still got together with Twiggy from time to time, once explained to me when I was a little girl just starting out, that the "skinny as could be" cutie from Kilburn, London, had started it all. All this "supermodel" stuff. Of course, no one back in the sixties knew who Lesley Hornby was, but *everyone* knew who Twiggy was, and the power of her one-name name made her as unforgettable as her huge eyes and her slight frame. So the fact that I was always "Deirdre," never Deirdre Flanagan, certainly enhanced my reputation in the business, as well as with the general public.

It's also fair to admit that I've benefited from certain other perceptions in a profession that's all about image. I was well known as one of the "big-timers" who never did skin-and-sex stuff. There were other girls, like Claudia Schiffer, who refused to sit for any kind of nudity, but I got a ton of press, both good and bad (which is also good) when it came out that I wouldn't even do swimsuits. (My old man would kill me! Not really, but he'd definitely hate it.) So it gave me a certain kind of nerdy, goody-goody cachet, not only with the public, but even within the business itself. I'd taken a stand, gotten away with it, and was generally respected for it.

Besides, underneath it all, I *am* a nerdy goody-goody.

What's wrong with that?

Some people, of course, naturally blamed it on the HSDD, which was also well known in the business, although it never leaked out, in any meaningful way, to the public. In truth, most of the people I worked with—clients, designers, photographers, stylists, dressers, etc.—couldn't have cared less if the pretty face they were working with had some kind of inhibiting sexual syndrome. In a way, it probably made their jobs a lot easier. After all, most of them were serious professionals who just wanted to get the job done, and get it done right.

Some of them, of course, felt sorry for me. Some of them envied me. Most of them didn't really care. So what? A few of the more curious might have taken a few moments to hop on the web and read about the "problem," not fully understanding it, then quickly forgetting everything they'd read, except for a few snippets here and there:

> *Hypoactive Sexual Desire Disorder (HSDD)*
> *a maladaptive sexual dysfunction cited in DSM-III-R*
> *the absence of sexual desires, including fantasies*
> *no libido, no sex drive*
> *either generalized (acquired) or lifelong*
> *possibly related to hormonal imbalance*
> *possibly related to excessive levels of prolactin*
> *the cause of lifelong HSDD is "unknown"*
> *sometimes difficult to distinguish from asexuality*
> *no current FDA-approved pharmaceutical treatments*
> *a few reputed "natural" herbal remedies, like Provestra*
> *believed to be more common than generally reported*

So *all* of these things, when combined, had created a very useful mystique about Deirdre (who was really just nineteen-year-old Deirdre Flanagan from St. Dominic's Academy). I suppose it didn't hurt that I also had a reputation for being professional, punctual, and always having an upbeat ready-to-work attitude. I'm generally full of energy, and just like my father, I like people. In truth, I've gotten along with almost everyone I've ever worked with, and on those rare occasions when I run into some kind of creep, I simply tell Sabrina about it, and I never have to work with that person again.

It's nice to be protected!

Eduardo was still clicking away.

Then I noticed that Carlos had entered the back of the studio. Carlos is one of those guys who's unaffectedly killer-handsome. Always. He was also my father's right-hand man at the gym, and I wondered what he was doing here at Eduardo's on Thirty-Ninth.

But I managed to keep my mind on my work.

Until the clicking stopped.

Eduardo lowered his Hasselblad and smiled.

"That's it, my dear," he said. "You were lovely, as always."

Eduardo always called me "my dear," and I liked it. It felt like family.

I stood up immediately!

Quickly!

My much-abused bottom, despite the heating pads, was still ice-cold and numb, so I rubbed myself a bit.

"Ooooo!" I exasperated, and everyone laughed, including Eduardo, including Carlos.

Then Eduardo, as he always did, stepped forward and kissed me on the forehead, just like he might have kissed one of his daughters. It was his way of saying, "Thank you."

Then as everyone began wrapping the shoot, Carlos came over.

"Hey, Popsicle."

I smiled, and he handed me a telegram.

"What's this?" I said stupidly.

"A telegram."

I was amazed.

"Have you ever seen one before?" I wondered.

"No. I didn't even know they still sent them."

"Me neither."

"It came to the gym, so the old man sent me over. I guess he thinks it might be important."

It was addressed to me.

I opened it.

It was a single word.

Unisphere.

I showed it to Carlos.

"What does *that* mean?" he asked.

"I have no idea."

"Who's it from?"

I shrugged.

Even though the other girls and I would often play little jokes on each other, this didn't feel like anything the girls would do.

Carlos was concerned.

"I don't like it."

Neither did I, but I didn't want to make a big deal of it.

"You meeting anyone later tonight?"

"No, Carlos. It's Friday night. After a quick stop at M&M's World, I'm heading home for a quiet night with the boys."

Meaning my old man and my uncle.

Carlos glanced around the studio, thinking it over.

"Fine, but I'm walking you home."

"It's not necessary."

"You carrying?"

"No."

"Then I'm walking you home."

That was the end of that.

By the way, did I mention that he's got a bit of a crush on me?

"I think *you* sent the telegram," I teased, "just so you could walk me home."

He smiled and shook his head.

In exasperation.

3. Makeup

I STARED AT MY FACE in the mirror.

It was early this morning.

Long before the photo shoot with Eduardo.

Long before the dead girl in Times Square.

I was (I am), I'd have to admit, remarkably beautiful, in a rather striking "Irish kind of way": well-defined cheekbones, clear-blue wide-set moist eyes, fullish lips, with a thick tumble of blackish-brown hair, without a trace of Irish red. The skin is perfect as well. Unblemished, unfreckled, and Irish fair. But never pasty, never overly whitish. Of course, like everyone else on the planet, my complexion suffers from natural dehydration, but I spritz my face regularly throughout the day, and it never tightens, dries, or (heaven forbid!) flakes.

My uncle once said that despite the longer and darker hair, I looked like a young Mia Farrow, with her similar suck-em-in, Kewpie-doll eyes.

"With more than a touch of Valli," he pontificated, "but of course, you wouldn't know who *she* was."

"Nah," corrected my old man, always disagreeing with his older brother about everything of minimal consequence. "She looks like Hedy Lamarr."

Then he turned to me, "Not that you'd know who *she* was."

So I looked them up: the young American actress who married Frank Sinatra; the Italian-Austrian beauty who'd starred in Carol Reed's *The Third Man*; and the famous MGM star, also Austrian, who'd come to Hollywood in 1938 to debut in *Algiers* with Charles Boyer. Then I studied every available beauty shot of the three actresses and watched their most famous movies, before deciding that I didn't look like *any* of them, even though all of them were undeniably stunningly beautiful.

"She's got a look of her own," Rexana responded seven years ago, dismissing both the disagreeing brothers, "and that's why this thing's going to work."

Meaning my modeling career.

Rexana, of course, was onto something.

For some inexplicable reason, I'd been blessed with a look that was all my own. It was, of course, entirely undeserved, and I've always been grateful, never forgetting the old adage, repeating it to myself every single morning:

> *What you are is God's gift to you;*
> *what you make of yourself is your gift to God.*

I stared at myself in the mirror, truthful about what I saw before me, equally aware of the twin traps of self-absorption and narcissism. I was also fully aware of the irony that *everything* I saw staring back at me in the mirror was *dead*. That no matter how beautiful I might appear in the glass, everything that I saw before me—the visible surface of myself, the top three layers of my five epidermises—was actually composed of dead or dying skin cells.

"Oh, well!"

I got to work.

With Lancôme Effacernes Concealer, I did my best to fill in the natural hollows of my cheeks. There'd of course be no blush today, so I overapplied Clinique Quickliner on my bottom lashes, emphasizing a "droopy" look. Then I covered the natural arch of my eyebrows with Paula Dorf 2+1 Filler and finished up with a bit of Chanel Hydrabase Ash-Colored Lipstick, left-to-right, right across the center of my lips.

In truth, it wasn't easy making myself unattractive, but I worked at it diligently. I tried to mitigate the perfect contours of my cheekbones, flatten out my eyebrows, unbalance my eyes, and uglify my lips. Today was my day off, at least until the shoot tonight with Eduardo, and I had lots of fun stuff that I wanted to do around town, so I did my best to "plain-ify" myself. As all my pals knew, as everyone in the business knew, I really didn't care that much for undue attention, and I certainly didn't want any males snooping around.

It was simple.

I had no interest.

Case closed.

Not that I blamed them. In the great scheme of things, it's their job, their preoccupation, their fundamental nature to be snooping around. On the prowl. But I wasn't interested, and I didn't want to deal with the distractions, so I did my best on my rare days off to make myself look as ordinary and inconspicuous as possible.

When my face was done, I frizzed up my hair a bit, parted it right down the middle, then pulled it back with a black elastic hair tie. Later, in order to conceal my figure, I pulled on my favorite baggy, ugly, off-the-rack, gray blouse, and left it hanging loose and untucked over a pair of oversized brown slacks. Then I slipped on my tan, horribly scuffed yet remarkably comfortable bowling shoes, and checked all the "use 'em as needed" props in my amazingly unattractive beige shoulder bag: a pack of stale Luckies that I'd bought two years ago, a depressingly ugly tan-gray scarf, a keep-them-away goldish wedding band, and a worn-down back-issue of *Heidegger Studies*, which I'd picked up at the Strand last year, with articles by people with names like Parvis Emad, Paola-Ludovika Coriando, and Jean Beaufret.

The absolute coup de grâce was my custom-made shades, with oversized, beige-brown, bug-eye thick lenses, and most horrifying of all, a dark bifocal line. Even though I had twenty-twenty eyesight and the lenses were nonprescription glass.

Who in the world would want to bother a girl who looked like that?

But males, as we're well aware, are extremely strange creatures.

Often, despite all my careful preparations, some of them would still come slinking around on my days off, trying to ruin my fun, so I'd be polite and friendly, but firm-firm-firm, quickly and clearly letting them know that they'd turned down a dead-end street.

Satisfied, I stood in the center of my large and well-lit makeup room, custom built by my old man and my uncle, and checked myself in the mirror.

I looked horrible.

I was perfectly satisfied.

Truth be told, I could do almost *anything* in this amazing room. To the right of my very expensive professional vanity with makeup mirror and table, there was a full-size Frigidaire refrigerator. To the left, there was a ceiling-high, open-shelved cabinet, and everything that I ever needed or wanted was either in that refrigerator or on those shelves.

Some of my favorites:

> *Smashbox Lip Enhancing Gloss*
> *Revlon Colorstay Lipsticks*
> *Nars Blushes*
> *Jemma Kidd Radiance Crème Highlighters*
> *L'Oréal True Match Powders*
> *Avon Retroactive Facial Moisturizer*
> *Elizabeth Arden Intensive Moisturizer*
> *Neutrogena Ultra Sheer Sunblock*
> *Kerastase Extra-Corps Hair Volumizer*
> *Clairol Nice 'N Easy Hair Gloss*
> *Rimmel Lash Maxxx Mascara*
> *L'Oréal High Intensity Eye Shadow*
> *Rescue Beauty Lounge Sheen Nail Polish*
> *Yves Saint Laurent Nail Lacquers*
> *Etc.*

The rest of my makeup room, except for the two floor-to-ceiling mirrors, was a surrounding succession of open closet racks crammed with my favorite clothes. There was also a large window in the room, looking over Forty-Eighth Street, and three carefully framed photographs: an old black and white of a youngish-looking girl in western clothes holding a Marlin 91 sharpshooter's rifle; a colorful action shot of the champ throwing a left in the Jamie Blacker fight; and a headshot, also in black and white, of a very beautiful young woman.

My mother.

4. Paris Café

A FEW HOURS LATER, I was sitting at my favorite table in the Paris Café reading the *New York Post*. I was wearing my "protective" wedding band, with the *Heidegger* journal and my pack of stale butts lying on top of the table next to my just-finished, mixed-greens salad. Nearby, on the bread plate, there were twenty-four M&Ms—yellow, orange, brown, green, blue, and red—waiting happily in six neat, color-coded rows of four.

The *Post* article was a follow-up about the final sentencing of the sick monster who'd stalked and killed Cindy Adams right across the river in Brooklyn Heights. Cindy had worked for Wilhelmina Models, and I knew her from the biz, and I liked her a lot. I was naturally delighted to learn that Edward Kroetz was getting "life without," even though I would have preferred either the juice or the needle for a slime like Kroetz. Nevertheless, spending the rest of his life in Sing Sing would be no Sunday picnic, especially for a coward like Edward Kroetz.

Satisfied, I put down the *Post*, looked through the large window, and stared at the Brooklyn Bridge. Being a Midtown girl with Jersey connections, I was naturally partial to the George Washington Bridge, which lorded itself so majestically over the Hudson, but let's face it, who wouldn't also appreciate and admire the mesmerizing beauty of the Roeblings' masterpiece? The steel-wire suspension bridge seemed especially lovely today, on this sunny morning in June, from my isolated table in the Paris Café. I sat alone, undisturbed, beneath the tavern's post-and-beam ceiling, not far from its elegant U-shaped bar, surrounded by elaborately carved and polished woods, old blended bricks, and sparkling mirrors.

Despite the name, the Paris Café was far more Irish than French, and it was my favorite hangout at the South Street Seaport. Back in the days of the great schooners, the seaport was one of the greatest ports in the entire world, but now it was an upscale and touristy part of the city, as well as a haven for Wall-Streeters and the courthouse crowd. The whole area, especially Pier 17, was overflowing with countless restaurants and boutiques, but I always came back to my table at the Paris.

The restaurant had once been the barroom of the prestigious Meyer's Hotel, founded in 1873 by Henry Meyer, host to all kinds of people over the years, from Teddy Roosevelt and Thomas Edison to Butch Cassidy and the Sundance Kid, to Louis Lepke and Albert Anastasia.

And, most importantly, Annie Oakley.

I love this awesome city that I'd been fortunate to grow up in, and I've always loved its extraordinary history. I once wrote a paper about Meyer's Hotel for one of my night classes at NYU. While it was true that the good sisters at St. Dominic's Academy were very proud of my success as a model, they were, nevertheless, a bit dismayed that after graduating second in my class, I might never end up with a college degree. After all, *everyone* at St. Dominic's got a college degree, and they loved to brag about their one hundred percent success. So two years ago, I decided to matriculate at NYU as a part-time student.

"I suppose you'll major in criminal stuff," my old man figured.

"Well," my uncle contradicted, "that shows how much you know your own daughter. It's perfectly obvious that she'll major in theater."

They were both wrong.

I majored in history, with an emphasis on New York City, doing my best to squeeze in a class or two, here and there, around the many shoots, "come-sees," and fittings. At the present rate, I figured that I'd probably graduate in about four more years.

If that.

Now it was time!

I looked down at the little, button-like, oblate spheroids waiting on my bread plate. The reds were my favorites, even though, of course, there was no discernible difference in taste. The green ones, according to urban legend, were supposedly aphrodisiacs, and my girlfriends, aware of my "condition," had once given me a huge jar of "personalized" greenies with "You go, Girl!" printed on each and every M&M. As Renée, a thoughtful petite who worked for Elite Models, suggested cautiously, "Maybe this'll help."

I was glad that the girls and I could laugh about my condition, and Angie once admitted that she wished she had the same "problem." Nevertheless, after finishing off my jar of greenies, I had to report back to my pals that nothing had changed.

Like all my model friends, I took my profession seriously. I was long and lean, five foot ten, and perfectly trim. Dress size: four. But I also love chocolate. *Any* kind of chocolate. Whether it's Ghirardelli, Godiva, or Hershey. Whether it's supermarket kisses, stars, or nonpareils. But what I love more than anything else, by far, are M&Ms. So, every day, I allow myself to eat twenty-four. Never more. Never less. In truth, it was the absolute highlight of every day, planned out carefully on my schedule the night before.

I began by popping an orange into my mouth and looking past the cobblestones at the great bridge spanning the East River, luxuriating in the chocolate, the sugar, and all the blessings of my blessed life.

Earlier, I'd stopped off at the Police Museum, which was a few blocks away near South Street, so I could walk down the NYC Hall of Heroes. I made sure that I walked the hallway *every* month, remembering Sergeant Mendoza, whom I'd known as a kid, and paying my respects to Michael Flanagan, the great-grandfather that I'd never known, who was shot in the back in Hell's Kitchen while trying to help a battered woman.

Now, sitting in the Paris Café, eating my M&Ms, the other enjoyable parts of my day off were about to begin. In a half hour, I was scheduled to meet Sabrina right here at the Paris, which was always great fun. Years ago, long before she'd become a high-powered agent at Ford Models, Sabrina Sinclair had been a top-of-the-line model herself, especially favored by Armani and Oscar de la Renta. She was also, like me, a protégé of Rexana Rhodes.

Even though Sabrina sometimes seemed a bit flaky and spacey, underneath her upbeat rather dizzying exterior, she was absolutely the best booker in the city, and she did her best to protect me. Always. She knew exactly what I wanted, and she kept me busy, and she also arranged time for my "book outs," those wonderful blocks of hours and days when I took time off from my job.

Since I worked exclusively with Sabrina, we naturally talked on the phone several times a day, but I still looked forward to our "weeklies" at various restaurants around town, where we discussed strategies, the latest trends and gossip, and Sabrina's long-suffering love life. Now twenty-eight, Sabrina had already rejected thirteen proposals, but she was still romantically undaunted, always on the lookout. Sometimes she'd say, optimistically, "He's still out there; I've just got to find him!" On other days, she'd repeat like a worn-out mantra, the old saying, "Don't worry about finding the right man, just worry about becoming the right woman."

To which I'd always respond:

"You *already* are, Sabrina!"

To which Sabrina would shrug her shoulders, then tumble off into her next series of engaging non sequiturs.

Later, after my "weekly" with Sabrina, I'd be meeting up with the girls—Renée, Angie, Erin, Kim, Amber, and Suzi, all of whom were successful models—at the Westside Bowling Alley. Which might seem a bit incongruous, but that was *exactly* the point. None of us were especially good bowlers, not even me or Kim, who were supposedly the most athletic, but we greatly enjoyed each other's company and our few hours of bowling frivolousness. Modeling in New York City is a rough-and-tumble business, with lots of rejection, disappointments, and temptations, but I'd somehow managed to find and collect together this marvelous group of semi-normal "girls' girls," who just like me, worked relentlessly hard, kept their goals in front of them, and desperately needed some "girl time" at least once a week.

Later, after endless gutter balls, the "pamperization of Deirdre" would commence at Summer's Spa in SoHo. This was the part of my hectic profession that I most appreciated: a fully justified excuse to self-luxuriate with facials, manicures, pedicures, and most marvelously, a weekly Swedish massage from Inga Olsen, a forty-three-year-old mother of six from Stockholm, who knew how to pamper and tone and rejuvenate every single weary muscle in my nineteen-year-old body.

I placed the last M&M in my mouth, a green one, and I let it melt slowly. I closed my eyes and concentrated. I could feel the sugars sinking deeper and deeper into my tongue before wildly coursing through my veins and blasting into my brain, releasing a billion endorphins.

At least that's what it felt like.

Someone approached the table, and I opened my eyes. He was a male, mid-fifties, but someone I was delighted to see. It was Ian Walsh, the daytime manager at the Paris, who'd gotten special permission to take me upstairs so I could look at the room that Annie Oakley had stayed in over a hundred years ago when she and Buffalo Bill had quartered at the hotel while the Wild West Show was performing in the city.

"You ready, Deirdre?" he asked, politely.

Finally, the last traces of the greenie vanished from my tongue, as the sugars gently dissipated within my system, my very essence, flaming out like falling stars.

Just as beautiful.

I smiled.

"Now, I am."

5. Times Square One

CAPTAIN PATRICK FLANAGAN arrived at the scene.

My uncle.

He was dressed, as always, in his meticulous uniform as a junior beat-cop lifted the yellow crime scene tape on West Forty-Third so he could enter the cordoned-off area. The forensic boys and the photographers were finishing up, surrounded by a curious, horrified Times Square crowd, lurking and watching, hushed and respectful.

When he saw me, he waved me over.

Carlos came too.

For most of my uncle's career, he'd been stationed at the Fourteenth Precinct, better known as Midtown South. Last year, he'd gotten his two gold bars, and he loved his job. He was tough, smart, caring, and funny, and all the boys in blue liked him and admired him. As all of them knew, twenty-two years ago, when he was still a rookie cop, his young wife, Rebecca, had been crushed to death in a fluke platform accident at Grand Central. At first, it seemed as though he'd never "get through it," that he'd *never* recover, so he went back to live with his brother (my old man) at Flanagan's Gym on Forty-Eighth Street. In time, he *did* manage to get through it, and he still lived at the gym with me and my father. He remembered Rebecca every single day of his life, but now his life was his job, his brother, and his niece (me), whom he'd been trying to spoil ever since I was a baby.

And succeeding.

Nearly six feet tall, still wearing makeup from the Ralph Lauren shoot, I was hard to miss, and a few voices in the crowd whispered:

"Look, there's Deirdre!"

Surely they were wondering, "Why's Deirdre here?" But eventually, they probably assumed that I was a friend of the pretty girl in the beautiful red dress and that they'd read about it online tonight or in the newspapers tomorrow morning.

"Hey, Sweetheart," the captain said, then he nodded to Carlos.

"Hey, captain," I said, always glad to see him. "A jumper?"

"Rick doesn't think so."

"Where is he?"

"Up on the roof."

I nodded. I was definitely intrigued.

We walked over to the body.

The dead girl lay beneath us, oddly undistorted, with none of the usual contorted positionings characteristic of leapers. She was remarkably beautiful, wearing a red evening gown, lying as casually and comfortably on the street as if she were at home sleeping in bed. She looked almost normal, except for the large pool of darkish red, still-coagulating blood that radiated outward from her pretty face like some kind of bizarre halo.

"She's beautiful," I said softly, as if to myself, and both the captain and Carlos nodded in agreement.

Then for some inexplicable reason, I was overcome with a powerful wave of uneasiness, suddenly affected, uncharacteristically, by the tragic death of this strange young girl who lay before me. I did my best to fight it off, trying not to show it. Maybe it was because there seemed to be something familiar about the girl, as if I'd known her in the past. As if she might have been one of those eager new models I was always meeting at various castings and receptions around town. As if she might have been, years ago, one of the countless younger girls at St. Dominic's Academy whom I'd passed in the hallways. As if she might have been, also back then, one of the many young girls whom I'd competed against, both here in the city and over in New Jersey.

Whatever the reason, I felt oddly overwhelmed. There seemed to be an inexpressible void within my heart, as a depthless sadness, like nausea, instantly swept over me. Death, of course, is always sad, especially the kinds of deaths that I was accustomed to dealing with, but it was more than just that tonight. It was more than simply death itself, and I couldn't explain it to myself.

Finally, as if to distract myself, I looked closely at the dress. I knew it well.

It was a sleeveless jersey gown with gathered bodice, ruffled hem, and minitrain.

"Where's her handbag?" I asked.

"Up on the roof."

"Who is she?"

"There's no ID."

Which was certainly odd.

"Nothing? No wallet?"

"Nothing."

We stood in the silence a moment staring down at the dead girl.

"It's a Donna Karan."

The captain nodded.

"It's couture," I added.

My uncle was an NYPD cop, but he also knew something about the fashion world, and he knew that the word "couture" meant one of a kind.

I left it right there. I didn't bother to mention to either my uncle or Carlos that I'd worn that exact same dress on the cover of *Marie Claire* last fall, which had served as the lead-in to a Donna Karan photo shoot within the magazine. I also didn't point out that the dress had obviously been refitted to the height of the dead girl, who was probably two inches shorter than I am.

There was something else.

"She's wearing nothing underneath."

Which struck my uncle as very peculiar, but he didn't respond.

"Where's the glove?" I asked.

The dead girl had a red glove on her left hand, but nothing on her right.

"I don't know."

"Is it up on the roof?"

"I don't know."

I looked at my uncle.

"We need to find that glove," I assured him.

"I'll get them working on it."

I stepped back, then looked upward, past the still-glittering face of Times Square One, staring at the roof. Not surprisingly, I couldn't see Dempsey. I couldn't see anything. Then I turned around and looked north into Times Square, over the heads of the still-milling crowd, into the ever-swirling colors. But I couldn't see it from Times Square One.

I was thinking about M&M's World.

The Mars superstore at 1600 Broadway.

Which, given the circumstances, was perfectly ridiculous.

But something was off.

The girl had gone to the top of Times Square One at the very same time that I was finishing a shoot at Eduardo's, just four blocks away, getting a telegram about the Unisphere.

Then the dead girl, who seemed somehow familiar, who was wearing an elegant one-of-a-kind dress that had been originally designed and fitted with me in mind, leapt off the roof just as I was strolling through Times Square on my way to M&Ms World to check out the new T-shirts.

I caught myself.

Surely, I was just being foolish and self-absorbed. Surely, such thoughts were nothing more than some kind of silly narcissism, which was always, as I knew perfectly well, a danger in my chosen profession.

6. Rooftop

I WALKED PAST another dead body to the edge of the roof and stared down into the kaleidoscopic colors of the southern end of Times Square, which lay beneath me—GMA Studios, the Disney Store, Benihana's, the Hard Rock Café, and of course the tiny, still taped-off yellow rectangle twenty-five stories below on West Forty-Third.

I lifted my eyes and looked outward over the glittering city. The Paramount, where Sinatra had once performed for infatuated bobby-soxers; Viacom headquarters at Astor Plaza; the Sheraton New York; the famous Brill Building, the one-time musical center of the universe; and all the rest of it.

"It's very beautiful," Dempsey said softly, as if not to disturb me.

"It's very romantic," I responded, and I sensed that Dempsey understood what I meant and that it might be relevant.

Like Carlos, Detective Rick Dempsey, NYPD, Fourteenth Precinct, was in love with me. Sorry to put it so bluntly, but there's no reason to beat around the bush, especially with one dead body lying on the roof behind me and another dead body lying on the street below me. As a matter of fact, Dempsey had once told me that he loved me. It was unequivocal. Then he left it right there. He also made it perfectly clear that he didn't care about my "problem."

"If there really *is* a problem."

He was blunt, sweet, considerate, and loving, and most any other girl in Manhattan would have tumbled into his arms.

Not dumbbell me.

Rick Dempsey (and this was a good thing) had always seemed like a younger version of my Uncle Pat.

"But a hell of a lot tougher," the captain once decided, which I seriously doubted, not because I doubted anything about Rick Dempsey's capabilities, but because I knew from a lifetime of firsthand experience that there was nobody tougher on the planet than either one of the Flanagan brothers.

Rick Dempsey, just like his mentor, was wedded to his job and his precinct, but he was also a bit of an enigma at the Fourteenth. He'd grown up in the Bronx, then right after high school, he'd taken off for Washington, DC, with a full ride to Georgetown, where he'd excelled in politics, foreign affairs, and all the necessary prep courses for the US diplomatic corps. But when he graduated, when most of his DC buddies moved over to the State Department, Dempsey came back to the city and signed up for the academy.

His reason was clear and simple.

"Someone shot my aunt."

It was a messed-up, yet easily solved mugging near a midtown grocery store, and Dempsey's aunt had survived the assault without much repercussion, but Dempsey still wanted to kick some ass for a while, and he wasn't about to sit behind a clerk's desk in the bowels of the State Department.

Sadly enough, just like his mentor, Rick Dempsey had also lost a young wife. Her name was Nancy, and she'd died five years ago after a brutal and drawn-out war with breast cancer. Somehow, just like his captain, the protégé had survived, and ever since his earliest days on the force, Dempsey had proven himself to be more than just another tough cop, being ruthlessly efficient, highly intelligent, and as both my uncle and I knew from experience, compassionate as well.

Right from the beginnings of my rather peculiar "second vocation," Dempsey had been tagged by the captain as one of my two protectors (along with Carlos) and my permanent liaison with the department. Ever since, Dempsey had always been ready to help in any way possible, on any and every case that I chose to get involved with.

I turned to my left and looked down at the dead cadet. He was sitting in a rather comfortable position, wearing a pristine, well-fitted uniform, with his head slumped forward on his chest, with a large red-black and coagulated exit wound at the top of his head. The bullet, seemingly a .38, had clearly entered beneath his chin and blown out the top of his head. The weapon, a Ruger GP100, lay in his lap, next to his right hand. He was still wearing his perfectly white military gloves.

I looked down at the small red handbag lying next to the corpse on the floor of the roof. It was, as expected, Donna Karan, and it gave me a chill. It was exactly the same matching accessory that I was holding on the cover of last fall's *Marie Claire*.

Although tempted, I didn't touch it.

I knew better.

"What's in the bag?" I asked.

"Tissues, some lipstick, some eyeliner," Dempsey explained, clearly prepared, adding, "both Estée Lauder."

When I smiled, Dempsey shrugged. *Of course*, Dempsey knew the details. He knew that I'd come up on the roof and ask him the brand name.

"I'll have it waiting for you at the precinct tomorrow," he assured me, referring to the red handbag and its contents.

I nodded and looked back at the dead cadet, resplendent in his West Point dress uniform. Third class.

"His name is Mitchell Carlyle," Dempsey explained.

I was shocked.

"The senator's son?"

"Yeah."

"This is the big time," I said, thinking out loud.

Once again, Dempsey nodded.

I looked at him directly.

"What happened?"

Dempsey, in his usual right-to-the-point manner, told me what he thought. The kids had come up to the roof to look at the city night-lights. Maybe there was an argument. Maybe there was an accident. Then the girl fell or was pushed, off the roof, and the kid, crushed and guilt-ridden, shot himself through the head.

Of course, if that scenario were accurate, then we both knew that there was no reason for me to get involved.

Not with an accident. Not with a suicide. As sad as those things always are.

"But why would he bring a Ruger to a formal?" I wondered, assuming that the kids had been at some kind of formal ball earlier in the evening.

"Maybe he was showing off," Dempsey suggested, without much conviction. "Or maybe he knew that she was planning to break things off. Maybe he planned the whole thing. Who knows?"

"Not here, Rick," I decided. "It's too romantic."

"Maybe that's exactly what he wanted."

I didn't buy it.

"Did anyone hear the gunshot?"

"No."

I expected as much.

"What are *you* thinking?" Dempsey asked.

"Maybe the gun was in her handbag, and when they got themselves all snuggled together on the rooftop, staring out at the night lights, she slipped it out and shot her boy through the head. Maybe the whole thing was a setup from the beginning."

"Then why'd she jump off the roof?"

"Maybe she didn't," I continued speculating. "Maybe someone else was up here and pushed her off after the murder was done."

"That puts at least three people on the roof," Dempsey responded, incredulously, "and two of them were murderers!"

This time it was my turn to shrug.

"Whatever happened," I said with conviction, without evidence, "I don't think she jumped. Whatever she might have done up here on the roof, I think she was murdered."

"The senator's going to love all these theories," Dempsey said. "Let's just wait and see what forensics comes up with."

I nodded.

I knew he was right.

"There's something else, Deirdre."

He knelt down near the dead boy and gently propped up his face. There was a marking on his forehead. I leaned over and took a look.

2 AM

Probably a Sharpie.

Needless to say, it gave me the creeps, ripping a chill right through me.

Was this mess in Times Square related to my telegram?

"What do you make of it?" Dempsey wondered.

"I have no idea," I lied.

"Maybe something's happening at two a.m. tonight?"

It was a rhetorical question.

Dempsey gently lowered the boy's once-handsome face down to his chest.

Spooked, I turned around and looked over the edge of the roof. There was, of course, a lot more than just colored lights, theaters, restaurants, and touristy good fun down below.

I glanced at Forty-Fifth and Seventh, where Faisal Shahzad had parked his Nissan Pathfinder full of explosives on May 1, 2010.

I looked at the Park Central Hotel on Seventh, where the notorious mobster/gambler Arnold Rothstein, who'd "fixed" the 1919 World Series, was shot and mortally wounded on November 5, 1928. Which was, as it turns out, exactly twenty-eight years before Albert Anastasia of Murder Inc., of the Gambino Crime Family, was assassinated in the very same hotel, in the barber shop, on October 25, 1957.

I looked over at 147 West Forty-Third, the site of the old Metropole Hotel, where Herman Rosenthal, on July 21, 1911, was gunned down by several of Lieutenant Charles Becker's vicious underlings, which eventually led to Becker's conviction and eventual execution in a Sing Sing electric chair.

I turned away.

I knew too much about the history of this place, about the history of the entire city, both the good and the bad. But tonight, it seemed to me, there was something especially evil lurking out there, and it seemed to be entangling me within its web, so I was finding it more and more difficult to focus on the good and forget about the bad.

7. "The Case of the Crying Comedian"

M RS. ANNE GILRAIN, recently escaped from Glen Haven Sanatorium, where she'd been committed after a nervous breakdown and subsequent alcoholism, is currently sitting in Nico's Restaurant with her former lover, Charlie Hatch.

Then her husband, Tom Gilrain, approaches the table.

> Tom (firmly): *Come on, Anne. Let's go.*
> Charlie (angrily): *She's not going anywhere with you, Gilrain.*
> Tom (undaunted): *Oh, yes, she's going back to Dr. Iverson. Aren't you, dear?*
> Charlie (standing up): *Beat it!*
> Tom: *Stay out of this, Hatch. I'm talking to my wife.*

As things heat up, Rowena, a dancer who knows Charlie Hatch, is watching intently from across the restaurant, standing next to the bar at the bottom of the staircase.

Charlie (aggressively): *Talk fast because she won't be your wife much longer.*

Unexpectedly, inexplicably, there's a bizarre cut-away shot showing Rowena walking down the staircase to the same spot where she was just standing!

"There it is!"

The Flanagan brothers swigged at their respective Guinness bottles and laughed like teenage idiots.

"Play it back again!" the captain suggested.

The champ agreed, and he aimed the remote at the screen to run the show back so they could laugh at the filmic flub one more time.

It was Friday night, better known at the Flanagans' as "Perry Mason Night," and I was dressed for bed, wearing my comfortable M&M pajamas, sitting in the living room of our rather peculiar living quarters above Flanagan's Gym at 335 West Forty-Eighth Street, where I've lived my entire life.

This particular episode, "The Case of the Crying Comedian," was the fifth show in the fifth season, premiering on CBS on October 14, 1961. The boys had grown up watching the old Perry Mason shows in syndication, and by now, they knew every single episode backward and forward, and they'd (too often) recite the dialogue along with the various characters, which I'd found both distracting and irritating when I was a little girl, but nowadays, I often caught myself doing it as well. Naturally, the boys especially enjoyed the flubs, like the editorial discontinuity in the scene with Rowena, played by Sue Ane Langdon.

"She was born in New Jersey," my uncle pointed out pointlessly.

"Yeah, but she was raised in New York and Michigan," my father added, equally uselessly, motivated more by a sense of accuracy than by some kind of brotherly one-upmanship.

Of course, I already knew pretty much everything there was to know about Sue Ane Langdon, who'd appeared in two of Elvis's weaker films, *Roustabout* and *Frankie and Johnny*, and who'd been a regular guest star on many of the sixties' best TV shows, like *Bonanza*, *The Dick Van Dyke Show*, and of course, *Perry Mason*.

Overall, there were 271 episodes of *Perry Mason*, airing from September 1957 to May 1966, long before they started making Perry Mason made-for-television movies in 1985. Given that we watched a single episode every Friday night, it meant that it took us five years and eleven weeks to complete an entire Perry cycle, not counting the TV movies, which we never bothered with. Then immediately, we'd start all over again, occasionally taking a break to watch the 156 episodes of *The Twilight Zone* or the thirty-nine classic episodes of *The Honeymooners*.

When the "Crying Comedian" was over, we all discussed, at length, the quirks of the plot, which was about a stand-up comic, Charlie Hatch, who was trying to protect the woman he loved, the aforementioned sanatorium patient, Anne Gilrain. We discussed how Perry (Raymond Burr) had handled the case. How the episode compared to the other 270 episodes. Then we discussed each character, each performer, including Jackie Coogan in a supporting role, who was once, long before he'd ended up as Festus on *The Addams Family*, the most famous child star in the history of cinema, starring with Charlie Chaplin in his best film, *The Kid*, in 1921, etc., etc., etc.

On the surface, I'm sure it all sounds dreadfully boring: two aging widower brothers sitting around on a Friday night, endlessly discussing a black-and-white TV show from the early sixties, examining all of its useless minutia, all of its subtleties, all of its "fine points," and every single one of its conceivable tangents. But I *loved* our Friday night rituals, and every single week, I looked forward to spending this special time with the two wonderful loving men who'd raised me and watched over me my entire life. So every Friday night, unless I was out of town on a shoot, we sat right here in our living room above Flanagan's Gym, spewing out tons of useless nonsense.

Which always reminded me how much I had to be grateful for.

Of course, I didn't just sit there and listen the whole time. I was quite a "Perry" expert myself, and I generally served as the referee as well, as the presiding and deciding magistrate, in the endless good-natured debates that arose between the brothers.

"Ready for number two?" the captain asked the champ, who always nodded, "Yes."

Then Uncle Pat rose from his old, padded chair, ducked into our little kitchen, opened the refrigerator, and got out the last two bottles of Guinness.

It was a story I knew well.

The boys were in their late teens (Pat being nineteen, Sean Michael being seventeen), and they went out one night, and as was fairly typical, drank too much, and then as was also fairly typical, got into a parking lot punch-out with two tough Italian kids from Chelsea Park. When the cops showed up, they all scattered like rats, but the Italian kids got nabbed. So the Flanagan brothers went home, slept it off, and when they woke up the next day, they were both thinking exactly the same thing.

"We've got to make some changes," Patrick decided.

"You're right about that," Sean Michael agreed.

If the older brother was really going to be a cop, and if the younger brother was really going to be serious about a career in the ring, then they both would need to put the booze in its place.

Starting immediately.

Today.

They were fully aware that it was much easier said than done because they both felt the "Irish inclination."

"What should we do?" Sean Michael wondered out loud.

"We've got to put an end to it," Patrick decided.

"Cold turkey?" Sean Michael asked with natural incredulity.

They talked it over a bit.

In truth, there was little in the world that the Flanagan brothers liked more than an ice-cold bottle of Guinness, so after wrangling with each other and their consciences for about an hour or so, they finally decided that they'd allow themselves two bottles of appropriately chilled Guinness each and every night for the rest of their lives, except on fight nights.

No more.

No less.

Then they took a vow.

Which was something that the Flanagan brothers took *very* seriously. A vow was a sacred and permanent bond, being both a matter of one's personal integrity and a test of one's personal strength of will.

So that was that.

"Who *really* won the fight in the parking lot?" I'd tease them whenever the story came up.

"We did," my uncle would say without hesitation, "but they were a tough pair of Guinea bastards."

Then my father would look over at his daughter as if it pained him to have to correct his older brother.

"It was really more of a draw," he'd clarify. "The closest thing to a *real* draw that I've ever seen, and I'm sure, Sweetheart, that after those guys got run over to the precinct, they were soon back with their buddies bragging about how they'd kicked the asses of some pasty Mick punks from Hell's Kitchen."

"Well, maybe you're right about that," Uncle Pat would nod, making a rare concession.

So every Friday night, they drank their first Guinness while watching Perry, drawing it out as much as possible, then drank their second Guinness after the show, also drawing it out as much as possible. So far, they'd *never* again had more than two beers, two alcoholic anythings, on any single night, ever since they'd taken that vow thirty-one years ago.

Which, of course, gave me the idea for my twenty-four M&Ms—no more, no less—when I realized that I was just as addicted to chocolate (hardly a model's best friend) as the boys were to their Guinness.

As the Flanagan boys slowly worked through their second bottles, rattling on about Perry-this and Perry-that, I enjoyed myself immensely, even though I was distracted by the two messages.

And the two deaths in Times Square.

After all, I owed everything I had, everything I was, to my "two old tough guys" as I liked to call them.

But, of course, it was my father, Sean Michael Flanagan, who was *really* the tough guy, having won the WBC super-middleweight championship of the world twenty-two years ago when he crumpled a much-battered Jamie Blacker in the second round of their title fight at Madison Square Garden. Before that, the champ had also won the Golden Gloves at seventeen, barely missed the Olympic team in '88, then turned pro when he was twenty-one. He quickly racked up an unblemished 18–0 record and became world champion when he was twenty-five years old.

In New York City, being a boxing champion, or even just a contender, especially if you're Irish, makes you much more than just a famous athlete, and my father, from all accounts, very much enjoyed being a celebrity. Maybe too much. He never allowed himself to get sucked into drugs, and he always stuck to his two bottles of Guinness, and he didn't even party that late into the night, but he did like the ladies. A lot. And they liked him. He was stop-em-in-the-street handsome, with an easygoing, fun-loving personality, and a boxer's physique. So he dated them all, movie stars (like Juliette Binoche), Broadway leading ladies (like Jessica McDonald), debutantes (like Gloria Grayson), and of course, a slew of New York models, including Rexana Rhodes, whom he might have married if he hadn't married my mom instead.

Back in those days, Rexana was on all the important covers—*Vogue, Glamour, Allure*, and *Elle*—and all the important runways, but she was much more than just a pretty face. She loved the business, and once she'd signed her contract with the Fords, she never left the agency. She became close friends with Katie Ford and John Caplan, and now, as Ford's senior VP, she was heir apparent.

When I was a little girl, after my mother had died and my father ended up in a wheelchair, Rexana was very much part of our lives. Even today, the champ meets her every Wednesday night for dinner at Sardi's, and I've never figured out why they never got married, even though I've often wondered about it and even asked my father about it.

"We're just good friends, princess," my old man would say. Rather evasively. "*Very* good friends."

"Yeah, they're just very good friends," my uncle would agree.

Well, I never had *any* doubts that they were "very good friends." As a matter of fact, I've never seen a man and a woman who seemed to enjoy each other's company so much, and laugh so much when they were together, and seem to love each other and respect each other.

So what was the problem?

Maybe my father didn't think it was fair to Rexana, given his disabilities. Or maybe Rexana didn't think it was fair to the champ since she worked almost every single hour of the week at the agency, excepting a few hours for sleep and a few hours for their weekly at Sardi's. Or maybe they'd both just decided that what they had, whatever it was, was better than anything else they could imagine.

According to the Flanagan brothers, the first time that Rexana took a look at me in the cradle, she told the champ, "She'll be on the cover of *Vogue* someday."

Which seemed a bit of a stretch to the old man.

"She's only three weeks old, Rexana! And she's got a big round head."

"Yes, but she's adorable, and she's got the map of Ireland stamped on her face."

Despite the champ's wariness about the modeling profession, he trusted Rexana implicitly, and when I was twelve years old, I signed my first contract with Ford Models and started building my portfolio. Right from the start, I was highly motivated, and years later, for a reason that Rexana didn't know about, I was fully committed to making as much money as I possibly could. I *needed* money, and I had my reasons, which were known by no one, not even my father.

At the age of twelve, I found myself, still a freshman at St. Dominic's on Sixty-Eighth Street, cutting classes for upscale fashion shoots and working at the same famous agency as a rather breathtaking list of legendary forerunners:

Maud Adams
Wilhelmina Cooper
Peggy Lipton
Suzy Chaffee
Cheryl Tiegs
Christie Brinkley
Jerry Hall
Carol Alt
Kim Alexis
Elle MacPherson
Christy Turlington

And, of course, *Twiggy.*

When the boys finished their post-mortem on the evening's *Perry Mason*, they started yapping about the current case. The real one. My old man was clearly concerned that the death of the senator's son made this particular case much too risky and high-profile for his only daughter.

"Besides, the poor girl probably jumped," the champ decided. "That's why she had nothing on beneath her evening gown. She was concerned that he might dump her after the dance, so she did her best to be as seductive as possible. She even conned him into taking her up to the rooftop, for the world's most romantic setting. But when he looked into her eyes and said, 'It's over, Honey,' she popped him through the head, then jumped off TS One."

"Wow, that's quite a pile of speculation," I kidded, "even for a master speculator like Sean Michael Flanagan!"

Of course, I knew what was *really* going on. He was worried about me getting sucked into a high-profile case.

"Not very likely," the captain quickly disagreed, surprising no one. "Personally, I think Deirdre's right. I think the little girl was pushed off the roof, and that puts the case right up her alley."

Because, as already mentioned, I only "take" cases, only "consult" on cases, as the brothers liked to call it, that involved the murder of young girls between the ages of fifteen and twenty-one. Those were my standard parameters, and the old boys knew them as well as I did, and they knew exactly how it all got started:

When I was eleven years old.

Eight years ago.

2008.

I was strolling home one evening from Sacred Heart, after skipping practice, carrying my schoolbooks. When I cut through one of the old cobblestone alleys off Fifty-First Street, I saw a dead girl lying on the ground beneath a fire escape. She looked quite peculiar, lying on her back, facing up. Death, with its rigid immobility, its finality, is always disconcerting, but she seemed quite content. Her eyes were closed, she had a little smile on her face, and oddly enough, there was very little blood.

Looking closely, it was clear that the back of her head had sustained the blow, the impact.

I glanced upward at the old fire escape, but somehow I knew, instinctively, that it wasn't an accident. It wasn't a slip. It wasn't a child's tragic fall.

It was murder.

I knelt down over the girl.

Very close.

There was a slight bruise on her left cheek and a distinctive candy smell at her mouth. It was both cinnamon and vanilla, which I'd never heard of before. Her lips seemed lightly covered with the redness of the candy, making them look a bit redder, although not that noticeable.

I looked over the rest of her, noticing several hairs, most probably dog hairs, at the hem of her skirt.

I stood up and looked around the narrow alleyway, which ran between two old warehouses, one looking vacant and the other apparently closed for the evening. I checked my watch. It was just past six o'clock. At the edges of the alleyway, there was some oldish debris, but there was also a single, fresh-looking, poppy seed hard roll. Which certainly seemed out of place, as if it had rolled to the side of the warehouse and was later forgotten.

I looked down at the dead girl again. She was, despite the increasing rigidity of her "deathness," quite pretty. She was dressed, like me, in a parochial school uniform, but she was definitely older. She was starting to mature, probably old enough for high school, maybe fifteen years old.

I'd grown up in a household (if you could call it that) with a detective uncle and lots and lots of talk about crime, murder, and detection, but I was still surprised that I had no visceral reaction to the dead girl's body. I was sad, of course. *Very* sad. But there was absolutely no fear, no flight impulse, no gag reflex. Instead, I looked her over, calmly and carefully, taking in every detail, touching nothing. Then stepping away from the body, I studied and memorized the entire scene.

Instantly, in those brief moments, I knew what I wanted to do with the rest of my life: track down the kind of perverted monster who could do such a thing.

It was too late to do anything for the dead girl, Mary Ellen Erickson, lying beneath me, but maybe I could find the predator who'd killed her. Better yet, maybe I could find *all* the predatory homicidal males who'd killed young girls.

Maybe I could establish some kind of justice in this world.

Like my uncle.

Like Perry Mason.

Not vengeance, but retribution.

Then I did what I shouldn't have done. I pulled down the fire escape ladder and climbed to the fourth story, the level below the roof, and looked down.

I felt a sudden whirl of vertigo, but it passed.

She lay beneath me, down in the alley, quite beautiful, smiling, with her eyes shut, with her reddish lips. Her arms were out at her side with the palms up and her legs were slightly, but definitely spread a bit.

In supplication.

In acquiescence.

She'd been posed.

At the time, I knew nothing about sex (the mechanics of which would have horrified me), but I was certain that the young girl's murder had something to do with sex.

I took out my cell phone and took some pictures before climbing back down to the alley. Then I called my uncle and waited.

When he arrived, with two uniforms, I told him, simply, "She was murdered."

He didn't dismiss it.

Then I said, "I want to help."

Oddly enough, he didn't dismiss that either, even though it was perfectly preposterous. Maybe he didn't dismiss it because he enjoyed nothing more in this world than spoiling his little niece whenever he could. Or maybe he didn't dismiss it because he knew, better than anyone else, even better than my old man, how my mind worked. Yes, I was still just a child, but he'd been watching me closely for eleven years, and he'd observed something that was still developing, something analytical, something speculative, observant, focused, maybe even creative.

Something which he felt was extremely odd.

Something special.

So he said, "Sure, Sweetheart."

Then he took me along when he went to interview the poor girl's family.

"Do you have a dog?" I asked.

It was my only question.

"No."

Then he took me to the morgue.

"Anything beyond the wounds from the fall?" my uncle asked.

The coroner shook his head.

"Nothing. No assault, no defensives, no sex. It looks like an accident to me, Pat."

"Was there anything in her mouth?" I asked.

The ME seemed more surprised by my question than by my peculiar presence in his freezer of death.

"Yes, a hard candy. Mostly dissolved."

"Can I see it?"

He stepped over to his work counter, found the see-through evidence bag, and handed it to me.

It was square, which seemed an odd shape for a hard candy.

"Thank you."

I handed him back the evidence.

"What about the hairs on her skirt?"

He was impressed, glancing over at my uncle.

"Dog hairs."

"What kind?"

He shrugged.

"Maybe German shepherd."

I looked at my uncle who knew what I wanted.

"Could you check on that, Albert?" he asked.

"Sure, no problem."

"Thank you," I said.

Then my uncle introduced me to a handsome young detective named Dempsey.

"This is Deirdre, my niece," Uncle Pat explained. "She's helping me work the case."

Dempsey smiled, and we shook hands.

But it wasn't a condescending smile.

It was a curious smile.

A friendly smile.

"Let me know if I can help," he said, and of course, he's been helping me ever since.

Then it was time to tell the old man, who, as might be expected, flew off the handle. It was the first and only serious argument that I'd ever seen the brothers have, and it frightened me, and I wanted it to end.

Finally, the captain, who was actually a senior detective back then, looked at his angry brother and said, "Maybe you should ask your daughter?"

Then he left the room.

So the champ did exactly what his older brother told him to do. He asked me what *I* thought, and I told him that "it," meaning this "crime-solving thing," was what I wanted to do more than anything else in the world.

He was incredulous.

(Who could blame him?)

"More than modeling?"

Which really hadn't started yet, and which at that point, was still just a little girl's daydream.

"Yes."

To this day, I believe that my single "Yes," my single unqualified affirmation, somehow assured the champ, with both sincerity and conviction, and he immediately backed down and gave in.

Eighteen years previous, *his* old man, "God bless his soul," didn't want the champ to turn professional and "get his bloody brains bashed in." What father would? But when they sat down in Clancy's Bar to talk things over, Sean Michael told his father, who'd been running Flanagan's Gym his entire adult life, exactly what it meant to him, so the old man shrugged it off and let it go.

Now it was Sean Michael's turn to shrug it off and let it go. If his idiot daughter thought she wanted to be some kind of detective, then fine. He wasn't about to get in her way. Besides, she was only eleven years old. Surely, she'd outgrow it. But sometimes, as his older brother regularly pointed out, the old man didn't fully understand his own daughter.

Later that night, I started "detectivizing" on the web. In a matter of moments, I discovered another girl who'd fallen from a fire escape down in Chelsea in a narrow alleyway. With cobblestones. Immediately, I emailed Dempsey and asked him for the crime scene photos.

Then I discovered that there was an actual flavor called "cinnilla," combining cinnamon and vanilla and that only one company sold it in squares. In Ireland! So I emailed Dempsey and asked him to find out where it was sold in Manhattan.

Then I lay in bed all night wondering how he'd done it.

How had he lured a city girl up on the fire escape?

I spent hour after hour speculating with the few facts that I had.

Maybe she was trying to help him?

Maybe he seemed harmless?

Helpless?

Lots of wild stuff, including silly stuff, whirled within my head, but I kept remembering that my uncle had once told me that Ted Bundy had lured his victims to his car by pretending to be injured.

Maybe the killer was waiting in the alley with a bag of groceries, pretending to be blind, with a Seeing Eye dog, a German shepherd. Maybe he pretended to trip, and the groceries fell all over the place, and the sesame roll rolled away. Unnoticed, forgotten. Then Mary Ellen helped him up from the ground and collected his other groceries.

"I'm fine."

"Let me help you."

"My apartment's on the fourth floor."

Which was really a vacant but furnished apartment, where he'd jimmied the front door earlier, then left it unlocked.

"Let's go," she said.

Something like that.

Then he gave her candy, forced her out on the fire escape, and pushed her off.

Then he went back down to the alley, carefully rearranging her body, placing it as he wished, covering as much of the blood as possible.

Then he went back to the fourth-floor fire escape, looked down, and saw the pretty smiling girl with her open, inviting arms.

Something like that.

Years later, my uncle told me what he didn't tell me back then. For good reason. Which was also never released to the press.

The semen.

When I told my uncle to have the forensic guys examine the fourth-floor fire escape, they'd found semen all over the place. As a little girl, I'd just assumed that he wanted to look at her, looking so pretty, from high above. I had no idea what he was really doing up there.

I'm glad that I didn't.

The next day I called my uncle.

"His name is Jackson Bruckner, and he's living at the Addison Hotel."

Uncle Pat, clearly taken aback, thought it over.

"He's got a German shepherd," I added, "and you'll find a white cane and dark shades in his apartment. Along with cinnilla candies and a lock pick."

"All right, Deirdre."

Bruckner was arrested forty minutes later.

Confessing seventy minutes later.

Earlier that morning, Dempsey had emailed me the candy list, which turned out to be rather short, just sixteen live-in residential hotels, mostly in lower Manhattan. The candy, as I suspected, wasn't sold in bodegas or supermarkets, which made things easy. Immediately, I started calling the hotels, faking my best big-girl voice, asking about the man with the German shepherd.

The Addison was the sixth hotel on the list.

Eventually, word leaked out about my involvement in the case, and both the press and the web went nuts: "Eleven-Year-Old Solves Erickson Murder." "Kid Detective Cracks Case." Etc. Stuff like that. As for me, I didn't enjoy it, *none* of it (my so-called fifteen minutes of fame), but I did, to everyone's surprise, agree to meet with the mayor for a photo op.

When I walked into Mayor Bloomberg's office at City Hall, he treated me just like any politician would treat an overly precocious eleven-year-old. He fawned all over me. I was invited to sit down in a chair that was much too big, and before the photographers were let into the office, the mayor, my uncle, and I bantered about the normally expected small talk: the case itself, the current heat wave, the Mets's losing streak. It was all very pleasant, and when it had run its course, the mayor looked at me and asked me exactly what I expected him to say:

"So, young lady, is there anything I can do for *you?*"

It seemed innocuous enough, but I was ready.

"I want a pistol permit and an investigator's license."

Poor Uncle Pat was shocked into silence, and even the mayor, a clever and effective politician, somehow *both* a Democrat and a Republican, was clearly taken aback.

Eventually, he decided to focus on the first part of my request.

"Have you ever fired a handgun, Deirdre?" he asked, with concern, trying not to appear too patronizing, trying to buy himself a little more time so he could conjure up a way to extricate himself from his awkward situation. After all, who wants to refuse the request of a little girl, especially the latest New York City hero, especially when the photographers are waiting right outside the door?

"Yes, Mr. Mayor, and I can shoot the lights out," I told him, in no uncertain terms.

I'm really not much of a braggart. Never, actually. The very idea repulses me, but I was willing to make an exception that afternoon.

It was clear to the mayor that I had no intention of letting him off the hook. Rather desperately, he looked over at my uncle.

For help.

He didn't get it.

"She's been shooting since she was ten, your honor, and she's a better shot than me."

The mayor nodded thoughtfully. It was clear that this wasn't going to be easy. Then he looked down at me, directly, and he tried another tack.

"But Deirdre," he said, reasonably, "you're much too young to have either a permit or an investigator's license. I'm sure you know that."

Everyone in the room, of course, knew that the minimum age for a gun permit in New York City was twenty-one, and the minimum age for an investigator's license was twenty-five.

"I know," I responded with a rather unnerving self-confidence, "but what I want is to have them both by the time I'm seventeen. Exceptions can be made in this state, and they've been made in the past, and I know you can arrange it. After all, you're the mayor."

The mayor smiled.

Wishing he was anywhere else in the five boroughs.

"You're right, young lady, I'll see what I can do," he finally decided, assuring me with a politician's "sincerity" that definitely wasn't what I was looking for.

"In my family," I explained, "we believe in vows."

"Vows?"

Rather helpless, the mayor looked over at Uncle Pat, but once again, he found no solace. The mayor was entirely on his own.

"If you're *really* going to do what you just said you're going to do," I continued, "then I'd feel much more comfortable about it if you'd take a vow."

Bloomberg was stunned.

He hesitated.

"It would make me feel much better," I assured him politely.

The mayor gave in.

He threw in the towel.

He raised his right hand, took a vow, and even said, "So help me God," that he'd do what he'd said he would do.

Six years later, on my seventeenth birthday, after helping my uncle with selected cases year after year, I got both my permit and my license.

Just like the mayor had promised.

Vowed.

The captain drained his empty Guinness, holding the bottle upside down in his mouth for about twenty seconds, coaxing out the last few drops.

Friday night was officially over.

I stood up, kissed my uncle, then kissed my old man, as they both whispered, "Sweet dreams." Then I went next door, into my strange little apartment, ready to relax in a luxurious bath of Epsom salts, before sneaking out of the house in the middle of the night while the brothers were off in dreamland.

8. Unisphere

AT 1:00 A.M., I snuck out the front door of the gym, wearing black Wranglers, a navy Lacoste Polo, and Sperry deck shoes.

Dempsey was waiting in his black Chevy Malibu.

He wasn't too happy when I called him earlier and told him what I wanted to do.

"Suppose I say no?"

"Then I'll call a cab or an Uber. I'm going, Dempsey, with you or without you."

I wanted his badge. I also wanted him to drive me, since I've never bothered to learn how. (I'm a city girl through and through.) I also wanted his protection. After all, if I'm honest about it, I'm just a skinny teenage girl, who despite a lot of martial arts training at the gym, has absolutely no illusions about her very limited physical strength.

What did Dirty Harry say?

"A man's got to know his limitations."

Something like that.

"Does your father know?"

It was a ridiculous question. Actually, it wasn't even a question. It was Dempsey's threat to tell my old man.

"He's asleep, and he doesn't want to be disturbed."

"The champ'll kill me."

He was right.

"Who's to know?"

There was a lot of dead air on my cell phone.

"All right, Miss pain in the ass."

"I've been called worse."

There was even more dead silence when I got in his Chevy. Immediately, we cut across nighttime Manhattan to the Queens Midtown Tunnel, then cruised along 495 toward Flushing.

Finally, Dempsey gave in.

"Why are we going to the Unisphere?"

I told him.

"I don't like it."

"That's exactly what Carlos said."

"You got your Glock?"

"Of course."

When we got to Corona Park, Dempsey pulled up to the guardhouse to alert dispatch that we'd be snooping around.

"Wait here."

I sat in the passenger seat, listening to the dispatch guy's television. I couldn't see the screen, but I could hear the hyperbolic reporting about an unidentified young woman who'd leaped, or been pushed, from the roof of Times Square One. So far, there was no mention of the senator's son.

Then there'd be a lot more hyperbole.

Dempsey came out of the station and got into the car.

"We're clear. Some guy named Parker is making the rounds, and he's been alerted."

"To what?"

"That some nutty nineteen-year-old wants to see the Unisphere at two o'clock in the bloody morning."

Dempsey looked down at a little colored brochure, with its little map. Then he restarted the car. I took the brochure and read it quickly as we drove to the Unisphere and parked about 120 yards away, hidden within the shadows of an overhanging stand of oaks.

We lowered our windows, waiting for we-knew-not-what, and stared at the Unisphere. It was quite a sight. Magnificent, in fact, and the night around us was cool and comfortable, and the moon, high above the city, was faint and mysterious, leaving dark shadows all over the grounds.

Except for Dempsey's hiatus in DC, he was pretty much a Bronx and Manhattan guy, knowing next to nothing about the other three boroughs.

But I did.

At the moment, we were sitting, metaphorically, in "the valley of ashes," as F. Scott Fitzgerald described the Corona Ash Dumps in *The Great Gatsby*. Fourteen years after the book was published, when it was time for the 1939 New York World's Fair, Robert Moses descended into the valley and wiped away all the ashes, creating an unprecedented wonderland in Flushing, New York, with the old Perisphere, the heart of the fair, constructed right here.

Then over two decades later, when they built the even more spectacular 1964 World's Fair on the very same city grounds, they'd placed the Unisphere on the exact same spot, on the exact same foundation, as the old Perisphere.

I sure wish I'd been alive to go to the '64 World's Fair!

(But then I'd be a lot older than my old man.)

I picked up the brochure again and read off a few pertinent facts for Dempsey:

twelve stories high (140 feet)
700,000 pounds
type 304L stainless steel
the world's largest global structure
designed by Gilmore D. Clark
donated to the World's Fair by US Steel
the symbol of the Fair
the symbol of the Space Age
which shows up in Men in Black
which shows up in Iron Man II

Dempsey laughed.

"It was dedicated," I continued, to "'Man's Achievements on a Shrinking Globe in an Expanding Universe,' and the theme of the entire world's fair was 'Peace through Understanding.'"

"It's hard to get any peace with you around," he complained, but we both knew he was protesting too much.

Behind us loomed the old New York Towers from the '64 Fair, and Mets's Citi Field was lurking behind the sphere. The National Tennis Center was somewhere off to our right, with the famous carousel off to our left, and the sailing marina on Willow Lake behind us, a bit to the left.

As the captain once told me after an evening Mets game, most of the criminal activity in Corona Park takes place near the southern wetlands, where vagrants often live in areas supposedly closed off to the public. Every year or so, there's a murder in the park, usually a mugging gone wrong, but that's to be expected in such a huge inner-city park, over 1,200 acres, stretching from Flushing Bay down to Grand Central Parkway.

"Where's Parker?" I wondered.

"They said he's on his midnight rounds, through the Hall of Science, the Wildlife Center, the skating rink, and the Art Museum."

"I love that place!"

"What place?"

"The Art Museum."

Dempsey shrugged.

"You've never seen," I asked, "the old Panorama from the '64 World's Fair?"

"Nope."

I was appalled.

"It's a huge scale model of New York City," I explained, fully exasperated. "It's supposedly the largest architectural scale model of any city in the whole world. It's great fun, Dempsey. I've come a bunch of times with the girls. You can search for the apartment buildings of all your friends and relatives from all five boroughs."

"Sounds cool."

Dempsey *never* uses the word "cool," so I wasn't sure if he was busting my chops or not. Before I could retaliate, we heard a noise at the entrance of the Art Museum.

Parker came out the front door, scanning his patrol card through an electronic keypad. Then he double-checked the doors behind him, walked over toward the Unisphere, glistening in the moonlight, and sat on the edge of the reflecting pool.

Right in front of the Sphere.

Facing us.

Off in the distance, he looked to be in his early thirties, lean, and despite his uniform, looking a bit worn around the edges. He was carrying a little brown lunch bag, and he took out a can of Coke Classic and a large hero. Maybe ham and cheese.

"Lunch break," Dempsey said, as if to himself.

"Maybe he got a message too?" I wondered.

"For what?"

"For me."

Dempsey checked his watch, but he didn't say anything.

The clock on his dash read 2:04.

So we sat there and watched Parker enjoy his midnight lunch.

Eventually, Dempsey got edgy.

"I'm going to check him out," he said, opening the car door. "Wait here."

I wish I had a nickel for every time Dempsey told me, "Wait here." But my uncle always insisted that I should do "whatever Dempsey says you should do."

I often did.

Dempsey, holding up his badge, headed toward the Unisphere. Parker was holstered, but there was no reason for any misunderstandings. They spoke for a few minutes, but I was too far away to hear anything. Parker seemed totally confused.

His cell phone rang.

It was extremely loud in the middle of the night, and I'd had enough of sitting in the car.

I walked over to the reflecting pool.

Dempsey was clearly frustrated by the fact that he couldn't hear the other side of Parker's conversation.

"Put it on speaker."

Parker did as he was told, placing the phone next to his can of Coke on the edge of the reflecting pool.

There was nothing but silence.

"Who *are* you?" Parker asked.

"*La Parca*," the man responded. "*La Muerte.*"

Spanish isn't one of my best languages, but I knew it well enough to recognize the figure of death.

The grim reaper.

Parker seemed resigned to whatever was happening.

"I don't think so," he said. "You're just the cleaning lady."

When there was no response, Parker, rather oddly, turned around and stared at the massive Unisphere looming behind him.

As if for the last time.

Then he turned around again, saying:

"You're nothing but a *marioneta.*"

A bullet immediately thumped into Parker's forehead, leaving a small black mark, as he slumped backward into the pool.

As I started to turn around and pull my Glock, I was immediately swept off my feet by Dempsey and thrown into the chilly waters of the reflecting pool. Dempsey came along with me, and we thrashed around a bit before we surfaced.

"Keep low!" he said.

Meaning stay behind the concrete edge of the pool.

I sloshed my way over to the right a bit, then peeked over the edge.

A dark figure was standing more than 250 yards away, off in the far shadows, impassively watching what he'd done. He had a scoped rifle in his right hand, maybe a Marlin 336, and he stood next to a black SUV, maybe an Escalade, which was facing in the other direction.

There was definitely somebody at the wheel, and the passenger side door was open and waiting.

The shooter wore black in the mostly black night, looking very much like the figure of *la Parca*. He was lean, maybe in his forties, maybe Hispanic, wearing a black sport coat.

Backlit by the moonlight.

There seemed to be no light within his eyes.

I pulled up my soaking Glock, shook off excess water, and fired. It was a difficult shot, at least 250 yards, within the darkness and shadows.

The figure buckled.

I immediately stood up for a better shot, for better balance, but he was already inside the black SUV, and it was driving away. I fired again, three more times, hitting the vehicle each time, but it kept on moving.

Soon it was gone.

I looked over at Dempsey. His gun was drawn, but he'd let me do the shooting. Then he called it in, gave a description of the car, and looked at me.

"At least, we got his DNA," I said.

Referring to the drops of blood I was sure were waiting on the ground 250 yards away.

Dempsey smiled.

"If only your groupies could see you now."

"You don't look so hot yourself, Dempsey."

He nodded, agreeing.

Then he started pulling the dead Parker toward the edge of the pool.

I guess I'd been so stunned by the suddenness of everything that I never had time to be frightened.

Then it hit me.

Hard.

9. Flanagan's Gym

THE BUZZER WENT OFF, the upstairs doorway opened, and I came down the stairs into the gym. It was exactly 6:55 a.m., just like every other morning, except Sundays, and I had to pretend I wasn't worn out from the night before.

I need my sleep!

I like my sleep!

Despite the hour, the gym was already in full swing, with the usual prework crowd training intensely. Over at Ring Number One, the champ was calling out instructions to Jimmy Carrillo, an eighteen-year-old welterweight prospect who could never seem to learn how to counter a right cross.

Flanagan's Gym was an old-fashioned fighters' gym, founded in 1919 by my great-great-grandfather from Ireland. Nowadays, most of the other New York City gyms—even Gleason's, the legendary gym that had started out in the Bronx, moved to Manhattan, and was now over in Brooklyn near the bridge—had been forced to start catering to the exercise crowd, including businessmen and businesswomen who saw boxing training as the best way to stay fit and punch away their stress, as well as the ever-increasing boxing-as-a-healthy-hobby crowd.

Even Flanagan's had a handful of those kinds of patrons, and they were always treated with respect, but it was really a fighters' club, where serious young kids from Harlem and Hell's Kitchen and the south Bronx could develop their craft, keep off the mean streets, and dream about fighting in the Golden Gloves. Maybe even Madison Square Garden. Sometimes, some of the "big boys" would stop by and train for a few days before their championship bouts in the city. Like De La Hoya, Cotto, and Bernard Hopkins in the old days. Like Andre Ward, Pacman, and Gennady Golovkin more recently. But mostly, Flanagan's was a friendly neighborhood gym for young kids who were serious about the sweet science.

When I came down the stairs, dressed exactly as I was always dressed, no one, with the exception of Carlos, looked in my direction. I was wearing my old-fashioned gray sweats, with a long-sleeve top, long drawstring pants, and a matching gray headband that held my tied-back hair in place. I was, of course, wearing no makeup, just a pretty girl in her floppy old clothes.

Down on the floor, I walked past the various mats and speed bags toward the northwest corner of the spacious gym, to a perfect square marked off by painted yellow lines, like a crime scene, as my old man liked to say. This was "Deirdre's Corner," and when the buzzer went off six mornings a week, everyone kept their distance.

I glanced over at Carlos, who was ready with the music.

Generally, although the kids were allowed to use their iPods, the champ liked to keep his gym music-free, except during my workout. At exactly 7:00 a.m., I took down my favorite Everlast rope, nodded at Carlos, and he hit the music button. Immediately, Shakira started blasting from the gym's corner speakers, and I began my routine.

Every day, the playlist was the same:

Ciega, Sordomuda
Tú
Que Vuelvas
Inevitable
Dónde Están Los Ladrones?
La Pared
Fool
Whenever, Wherever

Then there'd be a break, in silence, then the playlist would start over again. The entire workout took an hour.

Exactly.

I've been skipping rope ever since I was a little girl. What else could a toddler do in a professional boxing gym? Why not? It was the perfect exercise, and I was exceptionally good at it, and I loved it. I always felt sorry for people who dreaded their exercise routines. I looked forward to mine every single morning.

Even today, when I hadn't had a full night's sleep.

Quickly, I ran through my initial stretching exercises, then I began mixing intense one-minute skipping drills into my floor exercises and aerobic routines, gradually building the intensity of my regimen. About 7:25, when "Whenever, Wherever" was over, the music suddenly stopped, and Carlos came over to my corner with his stopwatch. Almost immediately, everyone else in the gym stopped as well, and they all looked at my isolated yellow corner. This was the only time that the boys in the gym were allowed to look in my direction.

The champ was a firm believer in discipline, and he ran a tough, tight gym. The rules were not only clear but they were also posted on the back wall in large black letters on a huge white sign, in between massive color pictures of Marvin Hagler and Julio César Chávez. Most of the Flanagan rules were normal stuff you'd expect in any gym: no booze, no butts, no PEDs, no spitting, no cursing, etc.

But there were also three "Deirdre Regulations":

13. No talking to Miss Flanagan.
14. No watching Miss Flanagan, except for her
   one-minute timing and her double Dutch.
15. No discussing Miss Flanagan.

Obviously, the last one was a bit hard for the champ to monitor, but the message was perfectly clear: keep your mind on your boxing and leave my daughter alone, or you'll get your ass kicked right out to the street.

Unfortunately, world records for skipping aren't as clear as they are in other sports, but it was generally accepted that the male speed record for sixty seconds was 241, and the female record was 208. Every year in high school, I'd been the all-city individual speed-jumping champ, and I came in third the only time that I went to the nationals in Philadelphia, when I was fifteen.

One time, I actually hit 200 skips, but it was unofficial, and I never really had any expectations about breaking the world record, but it still gave me something to shoot for. Just like the champ, who was now wheeling his way toward my corner, I believed in setting goals for myself.

When I was ready, everyone waited in silence. Aside from the champ and Carlos, there were, as was typical, about forty sweaty males training in the gym this morning.

Carlos looked at his stopwatch.

"Ready."

Pause.

"Go!"

For anyone who's never seen serious skipping, it's rather amazing how fast the nylon rope whirls around the jumper, who almost seems to be floating in the air. The rope is nothing but a blur, and even the rapidly bouncing feet are nothing but a blur. Even the soft clicking sounds of the feet on the mat seem to blur into an overall, lightning-fast, rhythmic, peripatetic hum.

When I first saw it on YouTube when I was a little kid, I looked at my old man.

"I want to do that."

He didn't blink.

"Why not?"

As you might guess, given my Flanagan genes, I was a natural athlete, but I was too tall for competitive jumping, and I knew it, and so did my old man.

"So what?" the old man said.

After all, every athlete has to overcome some kind of difficulty, so I agreed with the old man, and I never complained about it. Could I have cracked 208 if I was five feet two? Who knows? But I never even bothered to think about it.

Besides, if I were five feet two, I wouldn't have been a model.

"Thirty!" Carlos called out, marking the thirty-second halfway point as I pressed forward through the pain.

The guys in the gym, as was permissible, began to softly chant, "Yeah, yeah, yeah, yeah," to encourage my skipping frenzy. Eventually, the "yeah, yeahs" started picking up the pace, and it seemed that I did as well, even though it was probably just an illusion.

"Sixty!"

My minute was up.

Completely exhausted and covered with sweat, I stopped abruptly and tried to catch my breath. Everyone in the room looked over at the old man, who looked back at me.

"198."

Not bad.

The guys in the gym applauded, and two kids in Ring Number One tapped their gloves together. Everyone knew the stats. They knew that anything over 180 was distinguishing, and they also knew that no other woman in New York City, except for Kolbe Cortez back in 1998, had ever topped 192.

I nodded my thanks and gulped some Gatorade Perform 02 to hydrate myself as the boys in the gym returned to their business. A minute later, when my two-minute break was over, Carlos hit the music button again, Shakira was singing "*Ciega, Sordomuda*" once again, and I started the second half of my training regimen.

The only person exempt from the three Deirdre rules, as everyone knew, was Carlos Menendez, age twenty-three, born in San Juan, raised in Spanish Harlem. Who like Detective Rick Dempsey, was pointlessly in love with me, which was foolish for all kinds of reasons.

Carlos had been working at Flanagan's Gym ever since his family arrived in Manhattan when he was thirteen years old. He was now the champ's number-two trainer and his right-hand man, and he and I had grown up like cousins, if not brother and sister.

Carlos was also what all the girls in the borough describe as "perfectly gorgeous," with his Latin good looks, his heartbreak smile, and his tall, trim boxer's body. It didn't hurt that he was always polite and kind, being what all the girls called a "sweetie pie," and that he also had the hottest car in the borough: a cherry, vintage, jet-black 1973 Pontiac Trans Am 455 SD Firebird with a reinforced block, aluminum forged pistons, and a legendary "Screaming Chicken" decal on the hood in front of the scoop.

As a result, Carlos had broken a lot of hearts, not because he was reckless or indifferent, but because girls couldn't resist falling for him like a ton of bricks. They pursued him relentlessly, and he dated a bunch (maybe as the old man claimed, to get me off his mind), but nothing ever worked.

Just last week, Carlotta Hernandez had called me up and asked me to meet in the park near Greyshot Arch. Carlotta was a bright, *very* pretty, *very* lovely girl who taught middle school at St. Joseph's. I not only liked her, but I'd made no secret of the fact that I thought Carlos should marry her.

"He's broken it off," Carlotta said, "and we both know it's because of you."

She was crushed, and I wanted to help.

"I've made it perfectly clear," I assured her, "that it's never going to happen. I've known Carlos since I was a little girl. We practically grew up together. He's like family. He's like my brother, and that's the way it's always going to be."

Carlotta, of course, knew all of this already, and she knew that Carlos knew it as well.

"What's wrong with him?" she wondered, desperately befuddled.

"I don't know," I said. "It's some kind of infatuation."

"For ten years!"

I didn't have an answer, but I did want to make something perfectly clear:

"I've told Carlos numerous times that you two should get married."

Carlotta knew.

I tried again.

"Maybe he'll come to his senses and change his mind."

Neither of us believed it.

Finally, Carlotta stood up.

She wasn't bitter, and she certainly wasn't blaming me. She was just desperate, and she needed some girl talk, some commiseration, and she'd gotten a bit of both.

"Thanks."

It was sincere.

She kissed my cheek and wandered off into the park with that familiar Carlos-has-broken-my-heart look that I've seen so many times before.

Which wasn't *just* because Carlos was a "pretty boy."

When he was fifteen years old, he'd won the city's Golden Gloves, middleweight division, then the following year, he shocked everyone but the champ by giving up competitive boxing to continue his martial arts training in Krav Maga with a former Israeli commando, as well as training in Brazilian jiujitsu with the Gracie brothers.

"He's the most dangerous man in New York City," my Uncle Pat once said, which was exactly why Carlos had been assigned by my old man to be my "bodyguard," my "investigative assistant," whenever I was working a case.

"Don't you want," I once asked Carlos when I was twelve, "to fight at the Garden some day?"

"I just want to fight when it's needed," he said, which was an answer I much appreciated.

"Besides," Carlos added, "I've got my studies."

Which also didn't hurt with the ladies.

He'd gone to NYU, full scholarship, focusing on library science, with a minor in legal studies. He was also a natural computer whiz. Nevertheless, Carlos had no intention of becoming a librarian or a lawyer or a high-tech computer geek. What he wanted to do, aside from his work with the kids at the gym, had no real job description. No real job title or designation. Carlos liked finding things. Ever since he was a boy, fascinated with puzzles, he wanted to find things. Lost things. Important things. Personal things. Finding things not only gave him great personal satisfaction, but it also made him perfectly prepared for his assignment with me.

As a matter of fact, in all the years that I've known Carlos, I've only heard him brag once.

"I can find *anything*," he told me, with a mitigating smile, when I was twelve years old.

Which he could.

Which was probably a large part of the reason why Carlos had never believed the HSDD rumors, which we never actually discussed. As a matter of fact, we never actually discussed *anything* about Carlos's feelings for me, although I often made encouraging comments about his various girlfriends.

Like: "I think you should marry that one, Carlos."

Or: "She'd be quite the catch, Carlos."

Regardless, we both knew what we knew. We both knew exactly how Carlos felt, so we said nothing about it. But I knew for a fact that Carlos, always an intrepid researcher, had searched deep into the medical texts and come to his own conclusion that I didn't fit the "profile." For starters, it was a medical fact that women with HSDD typically have both serious stress issues and personal relationship problems, which clearly wasn't the case with me.

I was, by all accounts, remarkably well-adjusted.

Why shouldn't I be?

There were other red flags as well.

I don't believe Carlos ever believed that I had a "sex problem." Or a syndrome. He'd been watching me closely for over ten years, and I think that he felt I was just cautious and wary. After all, I'd been raised by nuns and two protective, fawning old men. As a result of my avocation, I'd seen much too much of the terrible violence that men (some men) will inflict on helpless young girls. I also knew better than anyone else, given my vocation, how looks like mine can get a young girl into trouble.

A few years ago, I overheard part of a conversation between Carlos and the champ in the old man's office. I only caught a few bits and pieces, but it was clear that Carlos was asking the champ about this "ridiculous" HSDD business. He seemed to think that the whole thing was a ruse of some kind (an admirable one) that had been perpetrated by the Flanagan brothers to protect their little girl. He also seemed to believe that I was a willing coconspirator—"if it wasn't her idea in the first place"—and that Rexana had cleverly floated the rumor throughout the modeling world when I was thirteen years old.

"That's a hell of a lot of conspiracy," the old man responded evasively.

Then Carlos noticed me standing in the hallway, and he shut the door, so I never knew if he got anything close to a straight answer from my old man. Well, Carlos was certainly correct about the *source* of the rumor, but it still didn't explain my apparent disinterest in men—or women, for that matter—or anybody else—and why I'd never had anything closely approximating a real date.

At exactly 7:50 a.m., Carlos and Eddie Mays, whose sister had been a legendary double Dutcher about five years ago in the South Bronx, came over to my corner with the longer ropes. When Shakira started "Whenever, Wherever" for the second time, all the guys in the gym took another quick break to watch my final three minutes of brutal double Dutch, bouncing relentlessly, seemingly effortlessly, off the floor, as if floating in midair within the two rapidly twirling nylon ropes that whirled around me.

When it was over, I stood in my corner, covered in sweat, waiting for my heart to decelerate. I was convinced that my workout was as intense today as every other day.

Surely, no one had noticed a thing.

"What's up?" Carlos asked, "Didn't you get enough sleep last night?"

10. Morgue

TYLER, THE CORONER'S ASSISTANT, opened the door to the refrigerated compartment, as a cool rush of rancid stink, the stink of death, flushed outward and engulfed me. When he pulled out the sliding tray, "Jane Doe" from Times Square was lying before me in all her pallid bloodlessness, in all her once-lovely nakedness. Without her red evening gown, the dead girl seemed terribly alone, abandoned, even pathetic, yet she was still lovely somehow.

Somehow familiar.

Captain Pat nodded at Tyler, and the young man left us alone with the corpse.

Once again, I was spooked by my overreaction. Over the years, I've seen countless dead young girls, all of them tragically, sometimes brutally, murdered, but this one, for some inexplicable reason, incited something far deeper than the normal sadness and the normal anger that I always experienced in this eerie, frigid chamber of death.

Whatever it was, I didn't attempt to figure it out, and I certainly didn't mention it to my uncle.

He knew anyway.

"What's up?" he asked. "You OK?"

"I'm fine," I assured him, "but this one, for some reason, breaks my heart."

The captain nodded. He felt pretty much the same. Then he remembered what Dempsey had told him earlier.

"Before the rooftop," he explained, "they'd been at the Sweethearts' Benefit Ball at the Waldorf."

I already knew.

Carlos had figured it out.

I nodded.

"What do you make of the letters?"

The dead girl had three tiny red letters, without periods, neatly tattooed into the flesh of her right breast, above the nipple.

BHC

The captain continued:

"Dempsey came up with 'Bellevue Hospital Center'; 'Black Hawk County,' which is in Iowa somewhere; 'Boston Health Care'; 'Benzene Hexachloride'; and oh yeah, '*Beverly Hills Cop*'!"

I had no doubt that Dempsey had been as thorough as possible. I leaned over the corpse and gently ran the tip of my forefinger over the dead girl's flesh, over the three little letters.

"It looks professional," I said, knowing it wasn't much help.

"Maybe they're a boyfriend's initials?"

"I doubt it. It looks like a fourth letter might have been removed, but I can't make it out."

"I'll have the pathologist check it out."

He looked across the dead body.

"Will you start at the Waldorf?"

"Not yet."

He was waiting for an explanation.

"It's all about the dress, of course. The dress is the key."

Meaning the key to the girl's identity.

"Of course, it is," the captain said, smiling a bit.

I ignored him.

"After I look it over downstairs, I'll run over to Donna Karan's showroom on Seventh."

I was fully prepared.

I was wearing a DK long-sleeve button-dress of lightweight white poplin, with a chest pocket, with a drawstring at the waist.

"Fine, but take Carlos along."

"I don't need Carlos to stop in a showroom," I complained. "I do it all the time!"

After last night, after the two messages, maybe I should have been warier. As already mentioned, I might be trim and athletic, with body fat hovering around the twelve percent minimum, but I wasn't especially strong. Yeah, I can shoot the lights out, but I was never going to overpower anyone.

I knew it, my uncle knew it, and the old man knew it.

But I didn't think anything was going to happen in the middle of the day in a showroom on Seventh.

"All right," he gave in, "but I'm not really comfortable with you working on a case when I'm out of town."

He was scheduled to leave this afternoon for a mandatory three-day captains' conference in Pittsburgh.

"I'll be fine," I assured him. "Dempsey and Carlos can take good care of me."

"They'd better."

He still didn't like it.

"You can call me for anything," he said. "Anytime."

"I will."

"*Anything*," he repeated.

"I will."

"And don't do anything stupid."

"When have I ever done anything stupid?" I kidded.

He gave an Irish shake of the head and rolled his eyes.

He nodded at the attendant, and Tyler came back across the room, then deftly slid the dead girl back into the darkness, into the frigid black interior feculence, as my heart shuddered a bit.

As the metal door slammed shut.

11. Donna Karan

A BIT MORE!"
I was extended outward, from the waist, hanging rather precariously off the edge of the roof of Times Square One, twenty-five stories above West Forty-Third. As best I could, with both hands, I was holding my Zeiss FL-LT binocs up to my eyes, searching methodically for the missing red glove, convinced that the inner-city wind had blown it against one of the nearby buildings last night.

"No way," Carlos said.

Firmly.

Carlos, of course, was holding down the back of my legs so I wouldn't fall off the roof, and he wasn't about to give me another inch.

"What's that?" I said, as if to myself, straining forward over the edge of the building for a better look. There seemed to be a distant splotch of red on the Barton Building.

Ignoring Carlos's concerns, I wiggled forward a bit, as Carlos, in response, tightened his already viselike grip. It may seem foolishly stupid, but I wasn't concerned in the least. There was no way that Carlos would let me fall off the top of a building.

"All right," I said, momentarily glancing down at the mad rush of midday activity in Times Square, suddenly realizing how precarious my situation really was.

"I'm coming back!"

I wiggled myself back a few inches, then Carlos slid his hands beneath my stomach, and with a sudden burst of strength, yanked me backward.

We both ended up lying on the black-tar floor of the rooftop. When I sat up and looked at Carlos, he was soaked with sweat.

"You're never doing *that* again," he said almost angrily. "Your father would kill me if he knew about this."

"Well, it's over now, Carlos," I said, trying to make light of it.

Which he wasn't buying, so I got back to business. "The red glove's stuck on a ledge on the sixteenth floor of the Barton Building."

I pointed across Times Square at the distant ledge.

"Can you get it?"

"Of course, I can get it."

"Then bag it and take it to Dempsey?"

He looked suspicious.

"Where do you think *you're* going?"

I stood up on the roof and smiled.

"I'm going shopping!"

So far, I hadn't told Carlos anything about last night's "activities" at the Unisphere, but he was sure to figure it out soon enough.

Right after the Parker murder, Dempsey and I were taken to the 110th Precinct in Queens and questioned for several hours. It naturally helped that Dempsey was NYPD, but the Flushing cops had their suspicions about the telegram, even though I showed it to them, not to mention the Sharpie message on the dead kid's forehead on top of Times Square One.

"So you decided to come to Queens at two in the morning?"

"That's what the message seemed to indicate," Dempsey explained, although it wasn't much of an explanation.

"A message from whom?"

Dempsey shrugged, then looked at me.

I shrugged a similar shrug.

Eventually, the guys from Queens seemed more than willing to leave the investigation with Dempsey and Midtown South, promising to send some blood samples to Manhattan.

About thirty minutes after dangling off Times Square One, I arrived at Donna Karan's showroom on Seventh Avenue.

I've always loved the DK line, and I've always loved Donna herself whenever we've met at various parties or receptions around town. I also liked her DK staff, from the designers to the receptionists, all of whom were polite and professional. Especially Angie, who was sitting at the main reception desk, doing her best to cover for Natalie.

"Sorry, Deirdre! Natalie'll be down in a few minutes. She told me to apologize profusely."

"No problem, Angie. I'll wait on the terrace."

After checking a few displays on the showroom floor, I made my way upstairs, stepping onto the elegant terrace overhanging

Seventh Avenue. I've always liked it up here, two stories above
the rush of the southbound traffic on Seventh, two stories above
the ever-flowing flow of the pedestrians down below.

I wasn't alone.

Off to my left, there was a stunningly beautiful Hispanic
woman wearing a striking green dress. She was staring out at the
city before us and holding a newspaper. She seemed lost in thought,
staring at the surrounding facades of the city's skyscrapers. She
appeared to be about thirty years old, and she wore her tight DK
dress in a way that seemed both elegant and erotic. Even somewhat
revealing. In truth, she had all the marks of the stereotypical Latin
bombshell, but there was also an undeniable sophistication and
grace in the way she carried herself.

And charm.

Suddenly, she seemed to break from her thoughts, and she
turned to look at me as if studying me closely.

"You're a very lovely girl," she said with a soft alluring
Hispanic accent. "I've seen your pictures."

She was confident and curious, with a remarkable self-
possession that also seemed a kind of detachment, a kind of
disassociation, which I found hard to fathom.

As for her compliment, I was, I have to admit, used to hearing
such things, and I responded, as always, politely and gratefully.

"Thank you. You're very kind."

The woman, as if searching for something, stared directly,
intently, into my eyes. Then rather abruptly, she turned again to
look at the skyscraper city.

"I love New York," she said, almost wistfully.

"Are you visiting?" I wondered, curious about where the
woman was from, but I didn't find out.

"Yes."

She held up the newspaper, the *New York Post*.

"I was *there* last night," she said, "in the crowd at Times Square. I saw the girl, and I saw you."

I was amazed. I tried to imagine what it must have been like for someone to travel to New York City, planning to have a wonderful time, then instead, ending up staring at the dead body of some mysterious young girl who'd fallen from Times Square One. The death of that poor girl, the "girl in the red dress," was all that anyone was talking about. Not just in the city, but across the country. The fact that she'd been out that night with a senator's son, who was dead as well, and that no one seemed to know who she was or what had actually happened, made it the lead story on all the news and gossip shows from *Dateline* to *Entertainment Tonight*.

"I hope it hasn't ruined your visit."

She didn't respond.

I felt I should say something more.

"It was terrible," I said, pointing out the obvious.

"She was a very foolish young girl."

Which seemed odd, cold.

She looked at me and added:

"Wasn't she?"

I didn't know how to respond. Maybe the woman had been traumatized by what she'd seen. Maybe she was upset because she assumed that the young girl had thrown her life away.

"Maybe," I suggested, "it wasn't entirely her fault."

The woman seemed unconvinced.

"Young girls are *always* at fault these days."

Needless to say, I was taken aback.

I was also irritated, so I decided to say nothing. Then, once again, the beautiful woman stared inquisitively into my eyes.

"They're *always* doing what they shouldn't be doing."

I began wondering if the woman's negativity, her cynicism, was the result of some kind of personal problem. Maybe a problem with a difficult daughter.

Despite my frustrations, I tried to be conciliatory.

"I suppose we *all* do foolish things sometimes."

"I suppose."

Then the woman in the green dress checked her watch, dropped the *Post* on top of one of the terrace tables, and changed the subject. Changing her demeanor as well.

"Didn't I see you on the cover of *Allure* last summer? Wearing Ralph Lauren?"

"Yes."

"You looked lovely."

"Thank you. I was very lucky. It was a lovely dress."

"You certainly are," she said oddly.

Then Natalie, chicly dressed as always, wearing a DK combo, came onto the terrace as the Hispanic woman looked at me one last time.

"*¡Buenos días, señorita!*"

Then she turned around and walked away.

Naturally, I wanted to ask Natalie, "Who *was* that weirdo?" but Natalie, flush with guilt, got to me first.

"Forgive me, love! We had a disaster upstairs!"

In the fashion business, as in all businesses, "disasters" were everyday occurrences, so I didn't bother to ask for details.

"No problem, but I need your help."

"Of course, whatever you want."

I pulled out a Xerox of the cover of last September's issue of *Marie Claire*.

"You remember this one?" I asked.

"Of course," Natalie assured me. "How could I forget?"

"Did the dress go retail?"

"No, I wanted it to, but somebody upstairs decided against it."

"Then where's the original dress? Did you sell it to anyone?"

She looked at me as if the answer was perfectly obvious.

"Of course."

"To whom?"

"To her."

"To whom?"

"That woman you were just talking to."

For a split second, it seemed as though all the traffic below on fashionable Fashion Avenue had suddenly stopped. That all the racing Manhattanites had frozen in their tracks. That even the white summer clouds had paused in the vast blueness of the New York City skyline.

An unsettling chill ripped up my spine.

"Are you sure?" I asked.

"Of course," Natalie assured me. "She's awfully hard to forget."

"Was she alone when she bought the dress?"

"Yes."

"Was it fitted?"

"Not here."

"What's the woman's name?"

"Margarita something," she responded, aware that something was wrong.

"Can you get me her last name?"

"Of course, Deirdre, but I'll need a few minutes."

"Fine. I'll meet you back here!"

Then I rushed downstairs and ran through the lobby past the reception desk.

Bursting onto Seventh Avenue.

I looked up and down the street for the distinctive green dress, looking north to Fortieth, then south to Thirty-Ninth. Seeing nothing. My heart was pounding. I felt uneasy, wary, and threatened.

I love this city, but ever since I was a child, I've been very careful about where I went, and when, but never at any time in my past had I felt so unsafe as I did right now.

I stood there all alone on the sidewalk in the midst of the never-ceasing flow of fast-moving New Yorkers, in a place that had always given me both a sense of protectiveness and a sense of comfort.

Not now.

I had the sinister feeling that I was being watched, that I was being manipulated, that I was being threatened, and it made me sick to my stomach.

Who *was* that woman?

12. Midtown Firing Range

I LOOKED AT the target.

Fifty meters away.

I own sixteen handguns, but the Glock 19 9 mm that I was holding in my right hand is my absolute favorite. It's a compact version of the G17, with a four-inch barrel, a ten-shot mag, and polymer grips. I love its heft, its balance, its adjustable sights, and its light recoil. I also love my "Baby Glock," a twenty-one-ounce version of the Glock 19, specifically designed for subterfuge, which I only conceal on rare occasions, and which I certainly know how to use.

I've been firing handguns at the Midtown Rifle & Pistol Range for nearly ten years, ever since my uncle gave me a copy of Glenda Riley's *The Life and Legacy of Annie Oakley* for my tenth birthday. That night, I read the entire book, got up early the next morning,

and went to the library to check out all the other books about Annie
Oakley, including the ones for kids and all the great picture books
like Isabelle S. Sayers's *Annie Oakley and Buffalo Bill's Wild West*.

Maybe it was just a sneaky ploy of my uncle's to get me interested
in firearms.

"A woman needs to know how to protect herself," he'd often say.

Or maybe it was a sneaky ploy of my uncle to offer up Annie
as a kind of role model, a kind of surrogate mother.

"She was a hell of a woman," he'd often say.

Or maybe it was just some book he'd picked up at random, in
the bio section of Brentano's on the day before my birthday.

Whatever the truth, I was hooked. I became instantly obsessed
with both the life and the character of Phoebe Ann Moses Butler,
and I still am.

I'd never known my own mother, and Annie Oakley, despite
fifty years of a happy marriage with Irish Frank Butler, had never had
children. But she adored them, always going out of her way to make
them happy, giving them her time, giving them all kinds of gifts.

When I was a child, I'd often imagine what life would be like
with a mother like Annie Oakley, whose close friend Fred Stone
once said, as did everyone else, including Buffalo Bill:

> *There was never a sweeter, gentler, more lovable woman*
> *than Annie Oakley.*

Whose husband Frank, in an early poem, had written about
the love of his life:

> *And you bet I love this little girl*
> *With the rain drops in her eyes.*

Of course, I didn't actually imagine myself walking down Park Avenue with Annie, then ducking into Saks or Lord & Taylor's. I also didn't picture myself out on the road with Annie, who often averaged about 5,000 miles a year, visiting more than a hundred cities. But I did imagine myself with Annie at the firing range. As well as helping her sew her soft cotton Western outfits. As well as sitting next to each other in some big bed somewhere talking about everything under the sun.

The champ, of course, knew about my childish fantasies, but he never discouraged them. He also agreed that Annie Oakley was "a hell of a woman," and he knew that kids have to dream their special dreams, just as he'd done as a kid, so he decided that my "Annie thing" was a good thing.

After all, Annie Oakley was much more than the quirky character portrayed in the popular musical. She'd come from nothing, from an essentially fatherless existence, working as a little girl at the Darke County Infirmary for Orphans, the Elderly, and the Insane. But she'd ended up the most famous woman in the world, the first female superstar celebrity, and a friend of kaisers, queens, Indian chiefs, and presidents.

She'd also entertained millions of people, both here and abroad, always giving everything she had. Even those people, who unfortunately, never made it to Madison Square Garden or Queen Victoria's Jubilee or the Exposition in Paris or the Columbian Expo in Chicago, could drop a nickel in a slot at the local Kinetoscope parlor and watch Edison's eight-second film of Annie firing off twenty-five dead-on shots in twenty-seven seconds with her Marlin 91 .22-caliber rifle.

After her death, the legend continued to grow: first with the movie starring Barbara Stanwyck; then with the blockbuster Broadway musical starring Ethel Merman, directed by Josh Logan, with music by Irving Berlin, produced by Rodgers and Hammerstein.

Was anyone ever the beneficiary of so much creative talent?

Then after all of that, there was the MGM version of *Annie Get Your Gun*, produced by the great Arthur Freed, starring Betty Hutton, who was filling in for Judy Garland. It was a film that I'd watched at least a million times with the Flanagan brothers, one which we all knew even better than the Perry Mason episodes.

Singing along with every song.

All of that stuff was interesting, but it wasn't what *really* interested me and the champ and Uncle Pat about Annie Oakley. It was the *kind* of woman she'd been, verified over and over by every single existing account. Raised a Quaker, reading her Bible every single day, being modest, humble, and kind. Yet also supremely confident, determined, and professional, with a will of iron. She also loved people—her family, her friends, and all the people who came to watch her perform in Colonel Cody's Wild West Show.

If I wanted to grow up and be like Annie Oakley, that was fine with the Flanagan brothers. *More* than fine. If I wanted, sometimes, to imagine that my own dead mother was, in some inexplicable way, just like Annie Oakley—or that Annie actually *was* my mother—they were fine with that too.

There were a lot worse things that a little girl could dream about.

Two weeks after my tenth birthday, the brothers bought me my first Glock, then they took me over to Westside Rifle & Pistol Range. They never expected that I'd become, like Annie, a "little sure-shot," or that I'd win a shelf full of ISSF and USAS trophies, but that's what happened, and they were fine with that too. If truth be told, the brothers were more interested in the fact that their tallish, skinny, gangly, attractive, but not especially strong little girl could now fire a pistol as well as anyone at NYPD.

Whenever it might be necessary.

I clicked off a cue in my head and fired.

It was always the same cue: someone was threatening either my father or my uncle. Occasionally, I'd substitute Carlos or Dempsey. I wanted to stay perfectly calm and ready if, at any time in the future, they might be in danger.

Any of them.

The Glock's 9-millimeters, all ten of them, fired with such rapidity that it sounded like a single, short, slightly punctuated pop. When it was over, I tapped the retrieval button and waited for my target. Then I heard the door opening behind me as Dempsey walked up to the firing line. I clicked the safety on my empty Glock, pulled off my Peltor earmuffs, and took out my earplugs.

"Didn't you take out your aggressions last night at the Unisphere?" he kidded.

"We were next, Dempsey."

"Yeah, probably. Where'd you hit him?"

"Upper right thigh."

Dempsey nodded, then he glanced over my shoulder at the tight cluster in the center of the target.

"Not bad."

"Number six seems to be wandering off by itself," I admitted.

He couldn't tell if I was serious.

"How could you possibly know if it's number six?"

He was incredulous.

"I know," I assured him. "Believe me."

Which he did, even though he also believed it was preposterous.

I started packing my gear.

"You know," he kidded again, "I like girls who can shoot better than me."

I played along.

"How many girls like that live in New York City?"

We both knew the answer.

"I also like girls," he continued, "whose favorite magazine is the Paladin crime catalog."

I smiled.

He was right. I always look forward to the new Paladin catalogs. After all, what girl in my kind of work, with an uncle at NYPD, wouldn't enjoy browsing through the latest books and videos about weaponry, combat, espionage, street survival, and all the rest of it?

"Yeah, Dempsey, I love reading my Paladin catalog every month, but it's *not* my favorite."

"What is?" he asked.

As he was supposed to.

"I thought *you* were the detective?"

He smiled, thought about it, then remembered a magazine that he'd heard me mention a ton of times.

"*Elle?*" he offered weakly.

"*Ring,*" I corrected.

"Of course, 'The Bible of Boxing.' Like father, like daughter."

I was ready to go.

"You finished babbling to yourself?" I asked.

He nodded.

He smiled.

Dempsey *always* smiled at me.

At everything I ever did.

13. Water Tower

WE CRUISED THROUGH the Lincoln Tunnel and took Route 3 west, avoiding the Turnpike. Sinatra was singing "I've Got a Crush on You," which I much appreciated. Dempsey, who was sitting comfortably in the driver's seat of his unmarked NYPD cruiser, was well aware of the fact that two of my favorite singers were Shakira and Sinatra. Since the flashy Colombian was a bit too much for Dempsey's taste, he'd bought a CD of Sinatra's *Reprise: The Very Good Years* and kept it handy whenever we were on the road together.

As we cruised west into New Jersey, I was busy checking the contact sheets from my recent "testing" with big-rep photographer Doug Rimmer. A few weeks ago, Sabrina had decided that it was time to update my portfolio, and I was glad to go along. So I was sitting in the front seat, with Dempsey's briefcase on my lap, leaning over the contact sheets, checking every print with my loupe and marking the shots I liked best with a small grease pencil. I did it quickly, with pleasure, with detachment, as if unaware that the pretty face staring back at me was my own.

Dempsey's cell phone rang.

He lifted it up, answered, and listened.

Which is illegal in New Jersey.

He told me that Carlos had retrieved the missing red glove from the Barton Building. Apparently, he'd walked more than twenty feet across a six-inch ledge, sixteen stories high, without a harness.

The glove still reeked with gunshot residue.

"She shot him," I said, matter-of-factly, still marveling at Carlos.

"Just like *somebody* suspected," admitted Dempsey, who was also impressed with Carlos.

I smiled.

Then I finished with the prints, put everything away, and sat back in my seat, listening to "Luck Be a Lady." We were now on the Parkway heading south and passing Nutley, New Jersey.

It was a long drive ahead to Atlantic County. Fortunately, Dempsey and I always enjoyed each other's company, whether we were listening to Frank or talking cases, sports, guns, movies, the champ, the captain, the precinct, NYC history, or Annie Oakley. As a matter of fact, over the past few years, Dempsey had developed a real fascination with Annie Oakley, and he was well aware of the Nutley connection.

In 1892, Annie and her husband Frank Butler, always dreaming of some kind of normal family life, built a permanent home in Nutley, New Jersey, thirteen miles from New York City, where she often performed. It was a handsome three-story, with double porches, located at 302 Grant Avenue, and for a while, at least, it gave Annie a sense of security and normality when they weren't on the road with Buffalo Bill. Eventually, a decade later, even though they'd made a lot of close friends in New Jersey, the house had become a burden, and they decided to give it up and move back to the city.

Into an apartment on Fort Washington Avenue.

I often wondered if the childlessness of her Nutley home had, in the end, made it too hard for Annie to endure. Of course, no one would ever know the truth since Annie Oakley, despite her well-known love of children, never spoke about such things. Which wouldn't have seemed proper. But at least, as I always reminded myself, Annie had something else that was very rare.

A fifty-year loving marriage.

Something that I'd never have.

"Why not tell me an Annie story?" Dempsey suggested, lowering the volume on "The Way You Look Tonight."

So I told him a story that maybe he knew already, but he listened anyway.

When Annie Moses was a little girl, she hunted game in the woods of western Ohio to support her mother and her siblings. Then they sold the game to a businessman named Charles Katzenberg, who shipped it off to various hotels in Cincinnati and Dayton, including the famous Golden Lamb Hotel in Lebanon, Ohio. As it turned out, the sophisticated diners at those various hotels would often compliment the chefs about the fact that their meals never contained "shot," which was a common and rather unpleasant occurrence back in those days. The reason, of course, was that little Annie Oakley only killed her game with headshots. Single shots. Right in the head.

Exactly as the chefs and the diners preferred.

Dempsey liked the story.

"Yeah," he said, rather thoughtfully, "sometimes headshots are necessary."

He wasn't thinking about game.

Then I asked Dempsey what he thought about the National League East, and we gabbed and gossiped all the way to the Jersey Shore, just like old friends.

Like brother and sister.

Earlier, at Donna Karan's showroom, Natalie had looked up the name of the woman who'd bought the red dress with a stolen MasterCard. The name on the card was Margarita Delgado, of Longport, New Jersey, a little beach-and-surfing town south of Atlantic City, at the southern end of Absecon Island. Maybe driving all the way to South Jersey was a wild goose chase since Dempsey could have easily asked the Longport Police to check it out, but both of us wanted to drive down and do it ourselves.

Just in case.

Eventually, after passing the glitzy casinos, we cut through Ventnor and Margate City and found the Delgado house at Twenty-Ninth Avenue south, off Atlantic Avenue, facing the ocean. It wasn't especially large, but it was attractive, pristine, and appropriately beachy. As Dempsey rang the doorbell, I stared out at the ocean. It was vast and spectacular and inviting, and I wished I could run across the beach and wade right in. I've always loved the Jersey shore (who doesn't?), with its cool-cold ocean water. I also love Atlantic City as well, having many fond AC memories, but today my oceanside trip was all about business.

A pleasant woman in her late fifties opened the front door. She was wearing a floral house dress, and she was, as I'd suspected, Italian, not Hispanic, which meant that the whole trip had been a waste of time.

Inside Mrs. Delgado's comfortable living room, she served her unexpected guests hyper-sweet lemonade, then explained, as we'd expected, that her credit card was missing, and that it was probably stolen about a week before she realized it was gone. When her monthly statement arrived in the mail, she noticed an expensive purchase at Donna Karan in New York City, so she called the people at MasterCard and they shut off her card.

"Was anything else purchased?" Dempsey asked, knowing the answer.

"No," she said, as if still surprised by the fact.

"Do you know *when* it was taken?"

"No, but I've been thinking a lot about it. For the most part, I've been at home over the past three weeks enjoying the beach, but I did go to Caesars about two weeks ago, and a few days later, I played some golf in Brigantine."

"What about New York?"

"Not in the past two months."

Dempsey nodded politely.

Then I gave Mrs. Delgado a well-understood look.

"It's right down the hall on the left, Hon," she explained, so I stood up and left the living room. I didn't really need a bathroom, but I wanted to snoop around a bit. Or, at least, get the vibe of the place, to see if anything felt "off." As I slowly strolled down the hallway, I checked out the two neat-and-cute bedrooms before entering a large dining room at the back of the house.

Then I saw it.

A gigantic smiling head looming over the entire neighborhood. It looked perfectly ridiculous, and I couldn't help smiling. Whether you like "smiley faces" or not (I do), this thing was perfectly adorable. It was the happiest water tower I'd ever seen, with its bluish tint, its extremely long neck, and its smiley face at the top, consisting of the familiar two eye-dots and curvy smile.

To get a better look, I stepped through the sliding glass doors onto the backyard patio.

Then I saw him.

High up.

In a lower rung around the tower's neck.

A dark figure, it seemed, was looking directly at me. Given the distance, I couldn't tell if it was male or female, but the position of its raised arms seemed to indicate that it was looking at me through high-powered binoculars.

Naturally I was spooked.

Threatened.

Invaded.

Creeped out.

Warily, I backed into the dining room, retreated into the hallway, and called for Dempsey.

"Look at this, detective."

Then I heard Mrs. Delgado's voice.

"Oh, she must have seen the water tower!"

She sounded perfectly pleased.

"Do you have binoculars?" I called out.

"Yes, dear," the woman answered, "I'll see if I can find them."

Dempsey came down the hallway, looked at me, and realized that something was wrong. Immediately, we walked through the dining room onto the back patio.

He looked up and laughed.

But I wasn't laughing.

"He's gone," I said.

"Who's gone?"

He sensed the edginess in my voice.

"Somebody was just up there, with binoculars, looking right at me."

I pointed at the first rung on the neck of the water tower.

Dempsey was confused.

"How could he get down so quickly?"

"Maybe he's around the other side. Maybe there's a ladder back there."

"Isn't he adorable," Mrs. Delgado asked, as she came up behind us and handed me the binoculars.

Dempsey nodded his thanks as I adjusted the binoculars and studied the distant water tower.

"Anything?" he asked.

"No."

I looked at Dempsey.

"There was definitely *somebody* up there, Rick, and he was looking at me.

"Maybe he was looking at the ocean."

"Maybe he wasn't."

14. The Waldorf

IS IT THE MOST elegant ballroom in New York City?
Maybe.

Is it the most elegant ballroom in the entire world?
Maybe.

Whatever the case, I've always loved the Waldorf Ballroom and everything else about the hotel, the legendary Art Deco palace at 301 Park Avenue. Where else could you walk into a hotel lobby and see Cole Porter's grand piano? Where else would Cole Porter have had his own apartment? Not to mention the Duke of Windsor, Marilyn Monroe, Douglas MacArthur, and Lucky Luciano? It was even the setting for one of my favorite guilty-pleasure chick flicks, J.Lo's *Maid in Manhattan*. (Even though they gave the Waldorf another name in the film.)

The only thing that I didn't like about the Waldorf was the old pretentious double hyphen, as in Waldorf=Astoria, which seems to have insinuated itself sometime before I was born, back in the sixties or seventies. It certainly wasn't there back in 1931 when the Waldorf Hotel was combined with the Astoria Hotel to become the largest and most luxurious hotel in the world.

Who cares?

I suppose a double hyphen isn't much to quibble about.

At the moment, I was waiting with Carlos in the Waldorf ballroom, supposedly modeled on the court theater at Versailles. The huge floor space was empty beneath its sparkling chandeliers, beneath its two tiers of elegant boxes.

"Not bad," Carlos whispered.

He'd never been inside the Waldorf before, not to mention the ballroom, and he was appropriately impressed. As for me, I'd been in the ballroom a number of times in the past: several charity balls, the Ford Models tribute to Eileen Ford, and the fortieth-anniversary celebration of Frazier-Ali.

But I'd never seen it like this.

Empty, yet beautiful.

The hotel manager, Anthony Beresford, entered the room, followed by six neatly uniformed members of his staff who'd worked at last night's Sweethearts' Benefit Ball for the American Heart Association. Beresford, I'd been told, always maintained an excellent relationship with NYPD, and he was more than willing to help the niece of Captain Pat Flanagan from the Fourteenth Precinct.

As they entered the ballroom, I noticed that one of the staff, a large, muscular, Hispanic man, probably in his late thirties, whispered something to Carlos in Spanish.

He seemed full of himself.

Carlos nodded.

Mr. Beresford looked at me.

"How can we help?"

I handed everyone a copy of a morgue shot of the Times Square Jane Doe, who'd now been identified as Lisa Livingston by several of Mitchell Carlyle's best friends at West Point. Then I passed around a sketch of "Margarita," drawn about an hour ago, from my best recollections, by Jenny Collins, the precinct's excellent sketch artist.

It was now time for some obvious questions.

And equally obvious answers.

Yes, they'd all seen Lisa last night, often dancing with a young man in a military uniform.

Yes, at least four of them had seen "Margarita" sitting alone in the northwest corner box on the second tier.

One of them pointed at the empty box.

"She was very beautiful," a female employee remembered.

Everyone agreed.

But *no*, none of them had actually spoken to the woman.

"Weren't you working that section, Jorge?" the manager asked.

"Yes, sir, but things were hectic up there." It was the large man who'd spoken to Carlos earlier. "She waved for more champagne once or twice, but that was it."

I didn't believe him, but I decided to wait.

None of them had seen Lisa and "Margarita" together.

"She just sat in her box and watched," Jorge added, trying to look helpful in front of his boss. "She seemed content. As if pleased to be alone."

That was it.

It was over.

I thanked Beresford, collected the photos and the sketch, then the manager and his six employees headed for one of the exits. The last to leave was Jorge, and he gave a knowing look to Carlos before he shut the door behind him.

"Where are we meeting him?" I asked.

"The north corridor."

A few minutes later, we found the north corridor, and Jorge was waiting.

Carlos didn't waste any time.

"How much?"

"A hundred."

Carlos took out his wallet and gave Jorge a hundred-dollar bill.

"It better be worth it," Carlos warned him, but the big guy wasn't intimidated.

"I'm waiting," I said.

"I saw the hot one in the balcony," Jorge explained, "talking to the soldier boy who shot himself."

"Tell me more."

"She asked about his father, the senator."

"What else?"

"That's it," he shrugged, with disinterest, with condescension. "It was just a bit of small talk, and it was over in less than a minute."

"Did Lisa introduce them?"

"Yeah."

"Where?"

"Up in her box," he remembered, as if completely bored, "the lovers went up there for a minute or two. That was it."

He assumed he was finished.

"What else?" Carlos asked.

Jorge shrugged.

"What was she wearing?" I asked.

"A low-cut gown. Some kind of yellow designer crap. Who cares?"

Carlos moved forward and stared intently at the man, who stared right back.

"That's not worth a hundred bucks."

"*Vete a la mierda, amigo,*" he said. "Now beat it, and take your *perra flaca* with you."

I knew what was coming.

I'd seen it many times before, although I never knew exactly *how* or *when* it would happen.

Instantly, the big guy was down on his knees, with Carlos, leaning over him, holding the man's head in some kind of choke hold. It happened so quickly, with such blinding speed, that even though I knew it was coming, I didn't actually see it. One moment, two men, who clearly didn't like each other, were standing in a deserted corridor of the Waldorf Astoria, and the next moment, the larger man was down on the ground pathetically gagging for breath.

Carlos, despite his usual kind and gentle demeanor, was, truly, as my uncle once put it, a very dangerous young man, and at the moment, I was wondering if he was a bit *too* dangerous. Jorge's face, contorted with pain, had flushed red with Carlos's unrelenting pressure. The man seemed to be a few seconds away from asphyxiation.

"Carlos," I said softly.

Carlos let up a bit, and the man glanced upward. All his smugness was gone, replaced with fear.

"Are you crazy?" he whispered, hoarsely, within his tightly constricted throat.

"What else?" Carlos asked.

Calmly.

"She called the girl '*sobrina.*'"

I'd spent enough time in my father's gym to know what that meant:

"Niece."

(After all, I was the captain's *sobrina.*)

"What else?" Carlos insisted.

"The lovers left early."

Which I knew already.

"What about the older woman?" I wondered.

"Yeah, her too."

"What else?" Carlos repeated.

The man shook his head rather helplessly.

Then Carlos looked at me.

"All right," I said.

Carlos released him.

Down on his knees, Jorge immediately slumped back against the wall, into a sitting position, and placed his hands over his throat, as if to comfort himself, as if to protect himself.

Carlos snapped his fingers in front of the man's face, and Jorge, startled, looked up at Carlos.

"If I find out," Carlos warned him, "that you know anything else. Anything significant. I'll be back."

The man shook his head warily, making it perfectly clear that he didn't know anything else.

Carlos was satisfied.

So was I.

As I turned to leave, Jorge suddenly cried out in pain as Carlos struck him a sharp blow at the side of his neck. Once again, it had happened too quickly for me to actually see it, but I knew what Carlos had done. I also knew that it wasn't like Carlos to be vindictive, but I also knew *why* he'd done what he'd done.

I knew what "*perra flaca*" meant, and to be honest, from my own point of view, I thought it was kind of funny that the big guy had called me a "skinny bitch."

Carlos, apparently, didn't think it was funny at all.

15. Gapstow Bridge

I WAS STANDING at the corner of Sixty-Sixth and Third.

Over two hundred and fifty years ago, when the road, the "thoroughfare," was still called "Post Road," the Dove Tavern was right across the street. On September 22, 1776, the provost marshall, with an escort of redcoat troops, led a young man to this exact same spot, allowed him to say a few words, then hanged him by the neck. Throughout the ordeal, the young man was calm, dignified, and eloquent. He had blue eyes and flaxen blond hair and was taller than most of his contemporaries. At the time of his death, he was a captain in the rebel army, a graduate of Yale, a former schoolteacher in his native Connecticut, and an American spy.

His name was Nathan Hale.

Today at the site there's no statue, no monument, just an inconspicuous plaque on the northwest corner to mark the young man's sacrifice. Nearby, an endless unknowing stream of Upper East Side traffic flowed by, as did an ever-flowing stream of equally intent, equally unknowing pedestrians. As for me, I was ashamed to admit that during my high school years at nearby St. Dominic's, I'd never even known that the execution site was only four blocks away. The only reason that I knew it now was because I'd written a paper about Nathan Hale's execution for my American Revolution class at NYU. I'd written about how Hale's famous "I only regret that I have but one life to lose for my country" speech had impacted the morale of Washington's battered and seemingly always-retreating troops in the early New York phase of the war. I'd also written about how Hale's death had had a telling impact on the execution of Major André in September 1780, after Benedict Arnold's shocking betrayal at West Point.

I was also fascinated by the long-standing debate in New York City about the actual site of the execution. Most historians believe (as I do) that it happened right here at Sixty-Sixth and Third, but there are other claims for City Hall Park downtown, where the great Frederick MacMonnies statue of Nathan Hale was erected in 1890, and there's another claim for Forty-Fourth and Vanderbilt, near Grand Central Station, where there's another plaque erected by the Daughters of the American Revolution.

I have *no* doubt that it had happened right here.

But that's the way it goes.

New York City is so replete with significant history that every street corner has a tale to tell, and no one can possibly know it all. I was doing my best. Doing so with wonder, with respect. As a matter of fact, I never visited this section of the Upper East Side anymore without stopping right here to reflect on the twenty-one-year-old captain, so young, who'd volunteered to sneak behind enemy lines to reconnoiter British troop movements in the city after the disastrous

Battle of Brooklyn Heights. The same young man, who'd been spotted by Major Robert Rogers of the Queen's Rangers, brought to General Howe's headquarters, sequestered for the night in the Beekman Estate greenhouse, callously refused both a Bible and a clergyman, and hanged the next day.

Sometimes I'd wonder what that exceedingly courageous and apparently quite handsome and athletic young man would have thought of New York City today. What he might have thought of me. A fashion model! A tiny cog in a seemingly unnecessary and possibly superfluous billion-dollar industry. Would he have thought I was perfectly frivolous? Maybe even pathetic? Maybe. Maybe not. Maybe the fact that I did my best to achieve some kind of justice, some kind of rectification, for helplessly murdered young girls might have influenced his opinion.

I hope so.

I strolled over to the park, greatly relieved that the "feeling" was gone. I was naturally creeped out by the current case, especially that peculiarly exotic woman I'd encountered on the showroom terrace, but at least I no longer had the feeling that I was being watched. It felt good, once again, to move within the always-comforting crowds of the city, walk across Fifth Avenue, and enter the Park at Sixty-Fifth.

Soon enough, I was comfortably settled in my favorite seat on my favorite bench in my favorite place in the whole city. In the whole world. It's true that I've always had a soft spot for Battery Park, especially in the evenings, especially in the rain, looking at the Statue of Liberty. I also loved the busy, bizarre, peacefulness of Washington Square, and I loved the Bethesda Terrace right here in the park.

But Gapstow Bridge is my favorite favorite.

Small wonder.

The little stone bridge, modeled on Ponte di San Francesco in San Remo, gracefully spans the northeast end of the Pond in a setting of bucolic rusticity and perfect tranquility. Complemented, oddly enough, by a spectacular city skyline, including the lovely Plaza Hotel looming above the bridge, above the trees, yet, somehow, almost miraculously, fully reflected in the waters of the Pond below.

It was always here, more than anywhere else in the city, that I came to relax and think, regardless of the weather, regardless of the season. Every day, back in high school, as I was making my way home from the academy, I'd stop right here in the park before heading over to Forty-Eighth Street.

Gapstow Bridge, of course, was hardly a secret. It was one of the most photographed places in the entire city, and it had appeared in countless TV shows and Hollywood films, maybe more than any other place in New York City. It served as a backdrop in *The Devil Wears Prada*, that nutty fashion-world film with marvelous Meryl Streep and charming Anne Hathaway, when *Runway Magazine* (which was obviously *Vogue*) commissioned a rather ugly "urban jungle" photo shoot in front of Gapstow Bridge.

As I carefully lined up my six rows of M&Ms, I was fine with sharing my bridge with fellow Manhattanites, tourists, film crews, or anybody else. Whether it was a bit overcrowded with sun soakers in the summer or empty in the chilling mists and blanketing snows of winter, the Gapstow always gave me a sense of peace in my life. It seemed perpetually lovely. Always. In a way that even seemed somehow romantic. I'd once read somewhere that countless marriage proposals had taken place right here, and I knew of at least one myself.

I popped a greenie in my mouth, luxuriating in the moment, in the pleasure, in the sugar. Then as I was checking my watch, I heard a chopper off in the distance. Slowly, the senator's helicopter was gliding through the cleared airspace toward the top of the Pierre across Fifth Avenue. I'd been debating with myself all day whether there was any point in crashing the press conference, but when I saw the chopper coming in, I decided to go. I knew that my uncle and my old man would be furious if they knew that I was out in the city alone, without Carlos, without Dempsey, but I felt safe again.

Besides, I had my weapon.

When I finished number twenty-four, my final red M&M, I stood up and made my way north of the Sherman Statue to Fifth Avenue. I had a fitting scheduled for later tonight at Calvin Klein's, so I was wearing a comfortable pink CK sheath dress, with a waist belt and a split neckline, wearing a bit of my "prettifying" makeup (not the "plain-ifying" kind).

At the entrance of the Pierre, I walked beneath the classic awning. Café Pierre had once been the hottest spot in Manhattan back in the forties and fifties, and Liz Taylor had once lived in the hotel in the sixties. Even today, the Pierre maintained an A-list clientele, and it was still remarkably beautiful inside. Since I already knew the hotel's layout, I wasted no time cutting through the elegant lobby, heading toward the Grand Ballroom, where I'd attended two weddings, a mayor's charity ball, and two upscale fashion-world receptions.

At the checkpoints, I was cleared rather quickly. I've got a very rare NYPD "consultant" card, signed by the mayor himself. It's a virtual open-sesame almost anywhere in the city. Sometimes the cops or security people would wonder why someone with a consultant card looked the way I looked, but if it ever became a problem, I politely asked them to call the captain.

I'd lived in the city my entire life, knowing hundreds of cops, including almost everyone at Midtown, and I seldom had a problem, even when I was carrying my Glock. All the Midtown boys knew I was the captain's niece, and they also knew that I was a model on the cover of some of the fashion magazines on the newsstands. As for why I was sometimes snooping around in police business, a bunch of them seemed to believe I was writing a department-approved book about NYPD. Surely it was a rumor started by my uncle. Others seemed to believe that I was interning part-time with Tony Arezzo in Midtown's crime lab.

The rest didn't seem to care.

At any rate, things went smoothly at the Pierre.

Despite heightened security and the presence of the not-so-secret Secret Service, I was soon cleared and entered into the crowded Grand Ballroom, which as always, was stunningly elegant. I'll leave it for others to decide which ballroom, the Pierre or the Waldorf, is more lovely, but I love them both.

This particular afternoon, however, the room was filled with nothing but sadness.

The senator's press conference was already underway.

He sat alone at a long table at the front of the room reading a prepared statement, with a concerned aide standing behind him. The room was crammed with the press (city, national, and foreign), and there were news cameras everywhere. It was also full of cops, mostly from the Nineteenth Precinct, and I recognized quite a few.

Alan Carlyle, dressed in senatorial blue, was obviously a devastated man. His son had died two nights ago in a bizarre, inexplicable, and sensational manner, and the boy's date, Lisa Livingston, who may or may not have killed him (or been killed by him) was still a virtual unknown, lying in the refrigerator at the city morgue. With difficulty, the senator explained that his wife was too distressed to attend, then he went on to say all the usual things that everyone expects in cases like these. He thanked everyone for their support. He asked for help.

For any kind of information. He mentioned the $50,000 reward, and he talked briefly about his son and his son's ambition to serve his country in the US Army. He also made it clear that he'd never met Lisa Livingston, and that she was, apparently, a new acquaintance.

Whatever one's politics, it was heartbreaking.

Not that the senator's politics were easy to define. He was a lifetime Democrat, but he was also a former DA, a high-profile protégé of Rudy Giuliani, and he was extremely tough on crime, a "hawk" abroad, and he often voted against his own party on some of the more controversial social issues. He was also married to Cindy Thompson Carlyle, a well-known and much-admired New York City socialite and philanthropist. He was universally regarded as a man of integrity, which certainly made him stand out from the majority of his senatorial colleagues, and all of these factors, combined together, made him perfectly electable in New York State, both upstate and down here in the city. In his two previous senatorial elections, despite taking the high road, he'd crushed his Republican opponents.

At fifty-five, he was a remarkably good-looking man, with brown eyes and graying hair. He was always perfectly neat and trim and dignified. Even now, in his desperation, Carlyle was, as always, never uppity or pretentious. There was quite a bit that I respected about the man, and if I'd come here this afternoon hoping to read something in his demeanor that might indicate some kind of unstated or unknown family problem, it was perfectly clear that it wasn't going to happen. I also knew that this was as close to the senator and his family as I was ever going to get, and he was revealing nothing relevant to the case except for his overwhelming grief and the absolute incomprehensibility of his loss.

Nevertheless, something didn't feel quite right. Maybe that's why I finally decided to come to the press conference. It was a nagging suspicion that maybe, just maybe, the two weird deaths in Times

Square weren't simply a lovers' quarrel gone wrong. That maybe they were really, in some inexplicable way, an attack on the senator himself. Surely, NYPD and the Feds and the Secret Service were all wondering the same thing, and now that I'd met "Margarita," I was certain that there was much more going on than just a pair of screwed-up teenagers.

Given my practical nature, I'm not much for conspiracy theories, certainly not political intrigue. But as the senator continued, I felt more and more uneasy. The man seemed much too vulnerable, so I started looking around the ballroom, checking out everyone who wasn't wearing NYPD, starting with the press, then hotel security. Eventually, off to my left, I spotted a tall Hispanic guy in a hotel uniform with a security badge. Like me, he was standing at the back of the room, and he was clearly packing. I looked him up and down, noticing the red stripes on the tongues of his shoes. He was wearing expensive Prada Monte Carlo sneakers with black leather uppers, with the signature red stripes on the tongues. No one who *actually* worked at the Pierre would wear rubber soles, no matter how expensive the shoes might be.

He looked at me and our eyes locked. He was expressionless. Unconcerned. I wondered if he was *la Parca,* the man at the Unisphere. Slowly, confidently, he moved away, moving down the right side of the ballroom, moving with a barely noticeable limp.

Casually, he moved past the TV cameras, heading toward the front of the room. Just as I was about to pull the Glock from my handbag, he took out a small plastic card, slid it through an unseen scanner, and vanished into a hidden security doorway. Following him through the crowd, I arrived at the doorway, but there was no doorknob, and I was unable to open it.

Terrified by what might happen next, I turned around, slipped behind the news cameras, and headed toward the stage. When the senator saw me approaching, he was confused.

He hesitated.

I called out to the Secret Service guys up on the stage.

"Get him out of here! Right now!"

Every cop in the room who didn't know me, of course, saw me as a potential threat, and several rushed toward me, as the senator's aide leaned over Carlyle. Instantly, from behind me, I heard two shots ring out.

Two quick pops.

Probably .38s.

The senator was struck twice in the chest. He slumped to the floor, surrounded by his staffer and Secret Service. When I turned around, I saw the security door closing again as several cops, too late, rushed toward the assailant. Once again, the door was locked.

In the ensuing panic, I was no longer the center of attention, and I quickly made my way to the other side of the room. I knew the Pierre pretty well, and I was certain that no one but a madman would attempt such a brazen assassination without some kind of escape plan. Nothing about this crime, or the ones in Times Square, seemed either unplanned or uncalculated.

As the pandemonium continued, I exited the left side of the ballroom and quickly made my way to a service elevator. Once inside, all alone, I looked at the floor buttons, wondering which way I should go. Then I remembered the chopper, and impulsively, I hit the button for the roof. Before the elevator doors opened again, I'd pulled my Glock from my handbag, tossed the bag aside, then hid myself, as best I could, in the front corner of the elevator near the button panel.

When it stopped, everything was quiet.

Too quiet.

Cautiously, I stepped into a narrow hallway, slowly moving toward the door at the far end of the corridor, which I assumed led directly to the roof. But I did wonder, since everything was so silent, if I'd taken the elevator in the wrong direction.

Then I heard two rapid gunshots beyond the doorway.

Suddenly, a huge man carrying a Taurus .357 burst through the doorway. He was at least six feet five, and he had a deranged look in his eyes as he was rushing right at me. I was terrified, but I had my Glock.

"Stop!" I called out.

He just kept coming.

Then I heard the whirl of the chopper blades outside.

I have an unwritten policy: no headshots unless absolutely necessary. So I fired a 9 mm into the man's left thigh, but it seemed to make little difference as he stumbled toward me. At the last second, I stepped aside, and the man crashed into the closed doors of the elevator and dropped to the floor in a heap. Cautiously, I stepped up behind him, noticing the entry hole in his back, then I leaned over and checked for the pulse that I knew would be missing. The man was already dead as he'd been rushing toward me in the corridor.

The door to the roof opened again, and a woman in a dark suit stood in the doorway. She was bleeding from her left shoulder, and she was terrified. Before she could shut the door behind her, she jerked forward at the sound of another gunshot, and a .38 slug blew out the front of her forehead and the woman's warmish blood sprayed across my face, as the dead woman fell to the ground.

I wiped the blood from my face, but I refused to stop and think about what was happening. Flushed with adrenaline, flushed with fear, I walked over to the roof's doorway, readied my Glock, and pushed the door open with my foot. Outside, the chopper was already rising into the New York City sky, leaving behind its executed pilot on the floor of the roof.

I rushed to the center of the roof, raised my Glock, but it was too late. The chopper was too far gone, already flying west over the park.

Exhausted, I sat down on the roof, checking, fruitlessly, for the pilot's pulse. Then I dialed 911 as I watched the chopper veer northwest over the park, as if heading for Morningside Heights.

All that my damaged, numbed, still-stunned mind would allow me to think about was that "this," *whatever* it was, was way too big for little me. It was definitely out of my league. A US senator had just been shot, and given where he'd taken the two hits, he was probably dead.

This was a case for the Feds, not a silly girl who liked to skip rope and pose for photographers.

Then I thought about my old man and Uncle Pat.

I was in a hell of a lot of trouble.

Big time.

16. West Point

I WAS STANDING NEXT to the statue of George C. Patton, waiting for my "date."

In the twilight.

I'd arrived at the Point a few hours earlier so I could have some time to roam around campus before slipping into my dress and fixing myself up at Callum Hall, which was across the street. Given the past few days, I much enjoyed my peaceful meanderings, checking out the monuments, stopping at the Gothic chapel, and visiting Trophy Point above the Hudson. It's hard to believe that this beautiful, bucolic, isolated campus, fifty miles north of New York City, had once been the most important fort in North America, and that a man like Benedict Arnold, whom Washington had trusted implicitly, would have attempted to turn it over to the British in 1780.

But he did.

And failed.

It was humbling to walk the same grounds once walked by the great Revolutionary generals: Washington, Wayne, Greene, Von Steuben, etc. And the place where later academy graduates had prepared for greatness: Grant, Pershing, MacArthur, Eisenhower, Patton, and Schwarzkopf.

But I was visiting the Point for something far less ground-shaking: Flag Day Hop at the famous Thayer Hotel. I'm not much of a dancer, but I love formal affairs, and I love the fact that the cadets still call their dances "hops." Even though the annual Flag Day Hop takes place in the middle of the summer, most of the cadets are still in the area at Camp Buckner, either undergoing field training or, if upperclassmen, serving as camp instructors. Flag Day is the perfect excuse to take some time off from the rigors of training, dress up, and go to a dance. In this case, the very same dance that Third-Class Cadet Matthew Carlyle had been planning to attend with his girlfriend before a Ruger GP100 had fired a .38 slug into his brain at the top of Times Square One.

Despite the Times Square tragedy, despite the astonishing assassination of Senator Carlyle yesterday afternoon, the Flag Day Hop committee had decided to proceed with tonight's formal. West Point, of all places, was familiar with soldiering on after tragedy and death. The Long Gray Line had lost 256 graduates in the Civil War alone, and it had a long history of surviving disasters.

The dance would go on.

I'd chosen to meet my date at this particular spot, next to Doubleday Field, because my great-grandfather, whom I never met, served in the "unstoppable" Third Army under George Patton, class of 1909. As a result, I'd grown up admiring Old Blood and Guts, and I've always loved this particular West Point statue of the General, as he stares intently ahead, most likely over some battlefield somewhere, probably North Africa, holding field binoculars.

Suddenly a sleek black BMW pulled up to the curb, and Third-Class Cadet John (Jack) Barclay from Bay City, Michigan, got out of his car. He was tall, handsome, and rather rugged looking. He was also, in the late-evening moonlight, perfectly resplendent in his West Point dress uniform.

Earlier this morning, before I'd been briefed by the Secret Service and the newly created task force at the Nineteenth Precinct about the senator's assassination, I listened as the champ talked on his speakerphone with Jimmy Leonard, an old boxing protégé from the Bronx, who was now the boxing coach at West Point, where the sweet science was still a requirement.

"I want somebody who's smart, tough, and already attached."

"Well, champ," Jimmy's scraggly voice said through the speaker, "the first two are pretty easy up here, but I'll have to do some double-checking on the 'attached' business."

"When I say 'attached,'" the champ clarified, "I mean already engaged or married. I don't want anybody getting ideas about my little girl."

I laughed.

My father didn't.

"I'll see what I can come up with," Jimmy assured him.

"Oh, yeah," the champ remembered, "make sure he's a yuk."

"Yuk" is the nickname for second-year sophomores at the Point.

"Great," Jimmy said sarcastically, "you want one with red hair too?"

The champ paid no attention.

"Get back to me before noon."

"Will do."

The two old boxers hung up simultaneously, and the old man looked at me.

"OK?"

"OK," I assured him.

The call came back within an hour. Jack Barclay was a yuk, just like Mitchell Carlyle, whom he knew quite well. He also had a fiancée who was off somewhere in Portugal on a Fulbright, so he said he'd be glad to take me to the ball and do his best to help me out.

Naturally, I was astonished that the Flanagan brothers were willing to let me go anywhere outside the gym without Carlos tagging along. Especially after what happened yesterday at the Pierre. But the captain, on the phone from Pittsburgh, had mulled it over.

Also on speaker:

"Maybe we *should* get her the hell out of town."

His brother was thinking the same thing.

"I could call Jimmy Leonard and have him find her some kind of tough-guy escort."

"Yeah, one of those cadets should be able to take care of her," the captain agreed. "Who knows, maybe she'll come up with something about the case."

"What about Carlos?"

"Have him drive her up," the captain decided. "Then he can go back and get her tomorrow morning."

There was a comfortable silence of brotherly agreement.

"When you getting back?" the old man wondered.

"I'm flying home tomorrow morning."

Although it was unsaid, it was perfectly clear that he was leaving the conference early because he was worried about me.

"Good," the champ said.

So the brothers were letting me go to West Point.

Carlos drove me north in his flashy Trans Am Firebird, and we had a good time together, quite a few laughs, despite Carlos's concerns about yesterday and his unwillingness to leave me alone at the Point.

"I don't like it," he said.

"I'll be fine," I assured him. "Now do what you've been told to do, and go home."

So Carlos went home. Then I roamed around the campus before dressing at Callum Hall. Now I was staring at my escort, Third-Class "tough guy" Cadet Jack Barclay, who as things turned out, was quite a bit more handsome than I was expecting.

I suppose it's fair to admit that he might have had a similar reaction to me.

I was wearing a gown that Sabrina had borrowed this morning from Calvin Klein. It was American-flag blue, floor length, with a pleated bodice. List: $2,197. I was also carrying a soft leather purse, American-flag red, from Dolce & Gabbana, similarly arranged at the last minute by Sabrina. List: $652. My shoes, matching blue Gucci stilettos, which could barely be seen, came from the Ford Agency closet. List: $658.

"Miss Flanagan?" he asked politely.

"That's me."

I smiled, and we shook hands.

"You look lovely," he said.

"Thank you."

"If my fiancée learns *how* lovely, I'll have some explaining to do."

"Then let's have some fun in the meantime."

"I'm good with that!"

He held the car door open, then quickly drove to the Thayer Hotel, where I'd checked in earlier when I first arrived. We made our way to the Crest Room, a large Victorian salon which overlooked the Hudson, which shimmered below in the moonlight. Everything in the room looked perfectly beautiful, elegant, colorful. American flags were everywhere. The cadets and their dates were dressed to kill, all looking marvelous. This year, Flag Day Hop had a fifties theme, and the band was thumping out a very energetic version of the old Buddy Knox rocker, "Party Doll."

For the rest of the evening, Jack did exactly what he'd been asked to do: guiding me from group to group, casually targeting all of Mitchell's closest friends. Of course, all of the partygoers tonight, when they weren't dancing and having a good time, were discussing the inexplicable and sensational murder of their fellow cadet and the assassination of his father, as well as the numerous conspiracy theories that were swirling in the press and whirling through the web:

> . . . *that Senator Carlyle had been killed by green*
> *extremists for his crucial vote on offshore drilling*
> . . . *that Senator Carlyle had been killed by Indonesian*
> *terrorists for his stand against aid to Jakarta*
> . . . *that Senator Carlyle had been killed by the New*
> *York mob for his earlier Rico busts of several figures*
> *in the Genovese family*
> . . . *that Senator Carlyle had been killed for his refusal*
> *to support Alan Sanderson for the Supreme Court*

There were salacious rumors as well, all rejected at the Point, that the two Carlyle deaths were in some way related:

> . . . *that the Carlyles had been killed by family*
> *members of Lisa Livingston, whom both men had*
> *been "sharing" sexually*
> . . . *that Mitchell Carlyle had actually set up the hit*
> *on his father, whom he hated, and then committed*
> *suicide before it took place*
> . . . *etc.*

All these inevitable discussions and speculations provided a natural segue for me to ask questions about both Mitchell and Lisa. As far as Mitchell was concerned, it was perfectly obvious that he was a much-beloved cadet, seemingly respected by everyone at the Point, and that he'd idolized his father. Mitchell was apparently a fun-loving kid, who never put on airs about his father's political status. He was also hardworking, always taking his military calling very seriously. He excelled at his studies, starred on the lacrosse team, and despite his lively nature, generally kept himself out of trouble. It seems that he'd only been hit with one "punishment tour" for some minor infraction. He was, it seemed, a true-blue, "Duty, Honor, and Country" cadet, and he was sorely missed by his friends.

On the other hand, no one knew much of anything about Lisa Livingston. Mitchell had apparently met her at some charity benefit in New York City that his family attended in April. He'd brought her to the Point only once, for the year-end hop at Eisenhower Hall. Everyone remembered her as being rather quiet, seemingly in awe of Mitchell, and he seemed equally impressed with her. It seemed to some of his friends as though they might be getting serious.

No one at West Point seemed to know that the two young lovers were planning to attend the Sweethearts' Charity Ball at the Waldorf, which was a bit odd, and no one gave the slightest credence to the idea that Mitchell Carlyle could have killed Lisa Livingston.

Or killed himself.

It was absolutely out of the question.

As I made the rounds, some of the partygoers, especially the girls, recognized me from the covers of the fashion magazines, which led to all kinds of pleasurable girl-talk about designers, makeup, other models, fashion gossip, etc. It also allowed me to get closer to Jennie Stevens, who'd been on a double-date with Mitchell and Lisa at the year-end hop.

"She didn't say much," Jennie remembered, "but she asked a lot about the Point. I suppose I did most of the talking."

"Did she mention the senator?"

"No."

"Did she mention her family?"

"No, when I asked her where she was from, she said Manhattan. That was it. No specifics."

"Anything odd?"

"Not really," Jennie decided, but then she remembered something. "You know, at one point, when we were in the ladies' room together, I'd left my handbag on the table outside, and I asked Lisa if I could borrow her cell phone, and she said, 'Sure.' When I looked at it, it said, 'Irina,' and I was a bit surprised, so I looked at Lisa, and I said, 'Irina?' and she just shrugged, 'Oh, yeah, that's my middle name, Lisa Irina.' I never gave it another thought until right now."

Jennie thought it over.

"Should I be telling the police?"

She was quite concerned.

"Don't worry about it, my uncle's the captain at Midtown, and I'll tell him tomorrow."

Then I showed Jennie the sketch of "Margarita."

"Have you ever seen this woman?"

She looked it over.

"Yes, on the night of the hop. I saw her standing near Battle Monument on Washington Road. She was dressed to the nines. She was unforgettable. *Very* beautiful."

"Did you ever see her with Lisa?"

"No," Jennie said, with another worried look. "Is all this stuff important?"

"I'm not sure," I admitted, "but I'll tell my uncle tomorrow."

She seemed relieved, then the band kicked off the final song of the evening, "Donna" by Richie Valens, so Jennie left to find her date.

Jack strolled over.

"Should we dance?"

"Of course!" I said, "as long as it's a slow one."

I stood up, took Jack's arm, and we moved to the dance floor. We danced slowly, comfortably, silently.

When the song was over, he looked at me directly.

"I know you're not done yet, Deirdre. You're up to something."

I didn't want to lie, so I shrugged.

"I promised your father," he reminded me, "that I wouldn't let you run around on your own."

I thought about it for a moment.

Why not?

Why wouldn't I want a West Point cadet helping me out?

"All right, Jack. I need to check out a few of the hotels in the area."

"Fine, I'll go get my car."

Earlier, when I'd checked in at the Thayer Hotel, I showed the sketch of "Margarita" to the manager and drew a blank. The same with his staff. Now I asked Jack to drive me to the Holiday Inn in nearby Fort Montgomery, which also led nowhere. Then we tried the Stilwell Inn, the Ramada in Highland Falls, and the Highlands Best Western with the same results. It seemed to be a waste of time, and it was getting late.

"What about Storm King Cabins?" Jack suggested. "They're a bit rustic, but they're first class and quite isolated."

So we drove up 218 to 9W, but I was uneasy. I'd been watching the side-view mirror.

"I think we're being followed."

"Really?" Jack said, as if pleased with the idea, glancing in his rearview at the headlights behind us.

"Pull off over there," I said.

Jack immediately jerked the steering wheel, swerving his BMW off the highway onto a dirt road next to a closed service station. Then he swung the BMW around to face 9W, as the car behind us, a silver Lexus, slowed down.

I pulled the Glock from my purse.

Jack was astonished.

"You know how to use that thing?"

"You'd be surprised."

But the Lexus continued up the highway, a bit too fast for me to catch the license plate number in the darkness.

Jack smiled.

"You're one hell of a date!"

I couldn't help smiling.

"It's not over yet."

We continued north to Storm King State Park and found the cabins. The check-in office was located in a small wooden cabin with a huge plate-glass window. When we got out of the BMW, I pressed the button for the night manager, and a young attendant, maybe twenty or so, suddenly appeared inside the office and opened the door. He'd probably been sleeping, but he took one look at me, and he shook himself awake, ready to help.

He stepped behind the counter, assuming that Jack and I wanted a room for the night, but I put a morgue photo of Lisa/Irina, along with the sketch of "Margarita," on the counter in front of him.

"Did you ever see these two?"

"Sure, about a month ago. This one's hard to forget."

He pointed at the sketch of "Margarita."

"This one was pretty too," he remembered, staring at the photograph more carefully, "but she looks like she's dead."

"She is."

"Whoa! What happened?"

I ignored his question.

"Can you look them up for me?"

"Sure."

The clerk slid the motel registration book across the counter and started flipping through the pages.

Jack interrupted.

He sounded serious.

"We've got company."

I turned around and looked through the large plate-glass window. There was a tall, dark, Hispanic man walking toward us, limping slightly, carrying some kind of semiautomatic, maybe a CZ-75. I'd seen him before, of course.

I'd shot him in the thigh at the Unisphere.

Then I'd seen him assassinate a US senator.

This time, however, he was coming for me.

I took out my Glock as the man raised his weapon, but Jack immediately grabbed me and pulled me down to the floor as a thunderous stream of 9 mm bullets blew out the glass and burst over our heads into the back of the office. I kept my head down until the magazine was empty. Everything was happening too fast, too loud, too surreal for me to panic, although my heart was slamming in my chest. When I lifted my eyes, I could see that Jack had been struck in the shoulder, and bright red blood was leaking through his gray dress coat.

It's weird how the human brain responds to fear.

For an instant, I remembered the frenzied scene in *The Godfather II* when Michael pulls Kate off the bed as the bullets blast into their bedroom.

Immediately, amid the broken glass and scattered debris, I rose to my knees, looking through the empty window frame.

The man was still coming.

Undaunted.

Without discernible emotion.

Or expression.

I wanted to shoot him in the head, just as Annie had done when she'd hunted game for her family's survival, but I didn't.

I shot him through the left shoulder, but the man kept coming. He seemed entirely unperturbed. We locked eyes as he raised his reclipped CZ-75. The look on his face seemed to say, "*Vete a la mierda*, Little Girl! If you really want to put an end to this, you'll have to do a lot more than a shoulder wound. You'll have to kill me."

So I did.

He was about to fire again, so I shot him through the forehead. Through the brain. He stopped where he was, a few feet away, staggered, then fell to the ground.

It was a headshot, and he was only the second man I'd ever killed. I didn't feel good about it, but it certainly felt good to be alive.

Eventually, the terrified young manager came around the side of his wooden counter, seemingly unhurt. As he did so, I noticed a set of headlights flash across the parking lot, as the car, the silver Lexus, drove off into the night.

I looked down at my date. Despite the blood and the hole in his shoulder, Cadet Jack Barclay seemed to be enjoying himself.

He looked at me and smiled.

"Nice shot!"

17. DNA

I was scheduled to do a "testing" in Brooklyn this morning with Reggie Westlake, to shoot some more headshots for my portfolio, but Sabrina took care of it. As it turned out, Reggie was perfectly willing to give his camera a rest, something about his thirteen-year-old daughter "acting out" at school.

Instead of posing in lovely Laurens, I spent the morning downtown in Federal Plaza talking to the Feds at the FBI Building on Broadway. They were surprisingly polite. No one lectured me about snooping around at the Point. They were genuinely relieved that I was OK, and they were eager to learn anything new about the case. After all, a US senator had been shot and killed, and the President of the United States had addressed it publicly in a press conference last night. Everyone in the law enforcement community wanted closure as quickly as possible, and now that the assassin had been identified and killed, the Feds were trying to figure out *why* he did what he did and *who* his accomplices were.

It turned out that the man who'd tried to kill me last night was a well-known thug from the DR who worked out of Atlantic City. His name was Antonio Salazar, who always worked with his younger brother Luis, who was most probably driving the silver Lexus last night and also driving the SUV at the Unisphere. The Feds picked up Luis early this morning at one of the AC casinos, but he'd lawyered up immediately with a pretty tight, though surely bogus, alibi. Even after the Feds ransacked the Salazars' condo, they came away with nothing, and Luis Salazar was already back on the streets.

After a quick slice (I know I shouldn't be eating the stuff!) at Ray's Pizza on Seventh, I spent the rest of the afternoon at the Nineteenth Precinct, going over exactly the same information with the NYPD Task Force. Fortunately, I knew most of the detectives in the briefing room, and they handled me with kid gloves. In truth, they seemed as concerned about my well-being as they were about the case.

Which I much appreciated.

Finally, it was time to head over to the Fourteenth Precinct and face Uncle Pat.

I took a seat in his office and waited as he stared out his window, looking over West Thirty-Fifth Street. There was a copy of the "Margarita" sketch on top of his desk.

"All I care about is you," he said, with more emotion than I was used to hearing from either of the Flanagan brothers.

"I know, Uncle Pat," I assured him. "I'm fine."

As odd as it seems, I really did feel fine. Whatever had happened last night had happened so breathtakingly fast that it seemed like a kind of out-of-body experience. As if it was over as fast as it had begun. It was like slipping on ice. It happened inexplicably fast. I'd reacted instinctively. And I'd come through it OK. Sure, I wasn't very happy that I'd killed a man, but I was glad that he was dead. He was the monster who'd killed Senator Carlyle, and Jason Parker, and maybe even the two kids in Times Square.

Then he tried to kill me.

So maybe I was safe, maybe I wasn't, but I certainly felt better about things.

"I should've never left town," the captain said. "It's all my fault."

Just as I expected.

"No, it's not," I said, as convincingly as I could, knowing that it wouldn't do any good.

"I should've never let you spend the night at the Point without Carlos," he continued, as if talking to himself.

"Even if Carlos had been there, nothing would have been any different. Except that Carlos would have been shot instead of Jack Barclay."

He wasn't paying attention.

He seemed oddly nervous, uncharacteristically edgy.

"From this moment on," he said, "Carlos is with you twenty-four seven. I don't care if it's a fashion shoot, a manicure, bowling with the girls, church, whatever. He's going along."

I didn't argue. Actually, I didn't mind at all. Besides, I had something else on my mind.

"Fine."

The captain picked up his phone.

"I'm getting Carlos down here right now."

"Fine," I repeated. "I'll be downstairs in forensics."

My uncle nodded, and I left the room and took the elevator down to the lab, thinking to myself, "What's going on with Tony Arezzo?"

Earlier today, while I was knocking off my verboten pizza slice at Ray's, I got a bizarre call from Tony.

"We've got preliminary DNA."

He seemed oddly nervous.

"Have you IDed the girl?" I wondered, hopefully.

"No."

I waited for more.

"What we *do* have is very preliminary," he reemphasized. "Remember that."

I was tired of waiting.

"What is it, Tony?"

"Your stuff's all over the place, Deirdre. Or at least, it seems like it so far."

I was confused.

"What do you mean?"

"We ran a ton of samples from the scene, both from the street and the rooftop," he explained, "and they called up *you*. All of them."

"Me?"

I was astonished. I'd been very careful, both down in Times Square and up on the roof, where I let Dempsey handle everything.

"Yeah, but it's just a partial match."

"Where?"

"On both of the bodies. Both the kid and the girl."

I was stunned.

"I never touched either one."

"I figured that," he said. "So it must have been planted. Which gives me the creeps."

"Me too."

There was silence on the phone line as Tony let me think things over.

I was baffled.

"I don't get it."

"Me neither," he agreed. "I tell you what, let me do some more double-checking, and we'll talk again this afternoon."

As I walked through the lab, I waved to a few of the techs and entered Tony's always-cluttered office.

He looked worried.

"I guess it wasn't a mistake?" I said, not wasting time.

"Well, it wasn't a plant either."

Which was even more confusing.

I sat down and waited.

"As soon as we're done," he said nervously, "I've got to go upstairs and tell the old man. He's going to kick my ass for waiting this long, but I wanted to tell you first."

I tried to be calm.

"Don't worry, Tony, just tell me what's going on."

So he did.

"It wasn't *your* DNA that we picked up on the initial sweeps. It was hers. It was Lisa's."

Which still didn't make any sense.

"Remember, Deirdre," he reminded me, "this is just a preliminary result. It'll take several days for a clarifying match."

"Come on, Tony, just tell me!"

"You and the dead girl seem to be a 'half-match.'" He hesitated a moment, then continued, "Do you know what that means, Deirdre?"

I was too astonished to have any other reaction than total bewilderment.

"She's my sister?" I asked incredulously.

"*Maybe*," he said, cautiously. Then qualified, "Your *half* sister."

I remembered the first time I looked at the dead girl lying in Times Square, in her beautiful red dress, and I remembered how the young girl had seemed, in some irrational way, oddly familiar. I also remembered staring down at the dead girl in the morgue, with my uncle standing beside me, and feeling overcome, inexplicably, with emotion.

Was it possible?

Was she *really* my sister?

Since Lisa Irina Livingston was clearly younger than me, that would mean that sometime after the death of my mother, my old man must have had some kind of romance, some kind of fling, and a baby girl had been born. I must admit, it seemed inconceivable that my father would have kept such a secret from me.

For my entire life.

The Flanagan brothers, whatever their multifarious and obvious flaws, were *always* honest, often stupidly honest, often to their own detriment. How could my father, whom I loved so much, have deceived me like this?

It didn't seem possible.

Then it dawned on me.

Maybe *he* didn't know either.

Maybe it was a one-time fling, and the mother believed that someone else was the child's father. Or maybe it was someone who didn't want the champ in her life back then, so she never told him about it.

"Did you know you had a sister?" Tony interrupted. Gently. He was still a cop, and he needed to know the answer.

"No," I admitted, "but maybe my uncle knows."

Arezzo nodded, thinking it over.

"Remember, Deirdre," he reminded me once again, "it's a preliminary finding."

But we both knew the truth.

Yeah, it's true that half sisters share only twenty-five percent of their DNA, but that's more than enough, even in a preliminary sweep.

We sat there in silence.

Tony was doing his best to be kind, to be patient, but eventually he needed to move things along.

"I've got to take this to the captain, Deirdre."

I nodded.

"*Now*," he said.

"I know. I'm coming along."

We rode the elevator upstairs in silence. My mind was racing, struggling to fathom how this case and all these terrible murders were somehow related to me. To my father. To Senator Carlyle. At the same time, I was trying not to think about the likelihood that my younger sister had been shoved off the top of a building in Times Square.

It was nearly five o'clock.

The captain was gone.

18. Jimmy's Corner

CARLOS ARRIVED at the precinct, and I asked him to call the gym. Which he did.

"He's not there."

Even Loraine, the captain's always-efficient secretary/assistant, had no idea where my uncle was.

"He just walked out of his office. Without a word."

"How did he seem?"

"Worried."

I looked at Carlos.

"We need to go to Jimmy's."

The captain wasn't much of a worrier, but whenever things got him down, he went to Jimmy's, drank a bottle of Guinness, and sat in the back of the bar with his problems.

Jimmy's Corner, on Forty-Fourth, was the last of the old-time old-fashioned boxing bars in Manhattan. Once a highly respected trainer and cornerman, Jimmy Glenn had worked a few corners for the champ back in the day, and his cozy, narrowish bar, with its walls completely covered with classic boxing posters and various other pugilistic paraphernalia, was always friendly and comfortable.

Carlos opened the front door, and we stepped inside.

Levi Stubbs, the legendary lead singer of the Four Tops, was wailing "Reach Out." The captain, just like his brother, loved Motown, and they especially loved the Tops.

"Jimmy's jukebox is the best in the city," one or the other would pontificate.

"Got that right," the other would say.

It was hard to disagree.

It was now early evening, and the place was packed with regulars, a few Yuppies who liked the feel of the place, and boxing tourists. Eddie Curtiz was running the Corner tonight, and he gave us a happy wave as we came through the door. Eventually, we worked our way to the bar, right across from Eddie.

"You missed the chief," he said with a smile, always promoting the captain to chief. Eddie was a likeable guy in his late thirties. The old man once said that Eddie was a "more than decent" welterweight back in his day.

"When did he leave?" I asked.

"About twenty minutes ago."

"Did he say anything?"

"Not really, he grabbed a Guinness and sat alone in the back until the other guy showed up."

"The other guy?"

"Yeah, some guy I've never seen before. Maybe fifty or so. He had the look of an off-duty cop."

"Did it seem prearranged?"

"Yeah, they seemed to know each other pretty well."

"How would you describe the other guy?"

Eddie shrugged, then did his best.

"Stocky, balding, maybe five feet eight, wearing dark blue sweats and a Yankees cap."

"Anything else?"

"Yeah, he had the Irish look."

"Was he packing?"

"I didn't notice, Deirdre, I was serving drinks at the time, but I'll tell you one thing, neither of them looked too happy. Which is weird for the captain, right?"

I agreed, nodding.

"He seemed troubled about something," Eddie added.

Well, I suppose it wasn't surprising, especially if he knew the truth about Lisa, and he was worried that everything would now be exposed.

Out in the open.

I thanked Eddie, then Carlos and I left Jimmy's.

After a couple of stops, I needed to get back to the gym. Where the old man would have to explain about my sister.

Or, on the other hand, where I'd have to explain to the old man that he'd had another daughter.

Who was dead.

19. Morgue

ONCE AGAIN, TYLER pulled out the sliding tray.

Before looking down at my sister, I glanced over at the Coroner's assistant.

"Thanks, Tyler."

He nodded.

Then he left me alone with the corpse. As always, he was polite and respectful, and I realized that I didn't even know if "Tyler" was his first name or his last name, and I felt guilty about it.

How little we know about those around us.

Those we work with.

Those we like and love.

I looked down at my "little sister." She looked very much as she'd looked a few days ago, yet somehow even *more* dead, even *more* refrigerated, even *more* vacant, even *more* frozen in her helpless and lonely nakedness.

Her face was still pretty. I could see some similarities with my own much-photographed face, the same similarities that I'd sensed the first night that I'd seen my dead sister's face in Times Square.

This was the little sister whom I'd never known, and my heart was crushed with endless might-have-beens. How we would have been the best of friends. How we would have been little gym rats together. How we would have worked out together. How maybe (who knows?) my little sister would have skipped over 208 skips a minute. Or how, maybe, she would have won the ISSF Junior Pistol Championships in Atlantic City.

I imagined just how wonderful it would have been to have had a sister, a companion, throughout my youth. Yes, I've been very fortunate to have many close friends in my life, at Sacred Heart, at St. Dominic's, in the fashion world. But I'd never had a sister. I'd grown up motherless and sisterless, and even though I never felt any lack of love from my father and my uncle, I still never had a sister.

I tried to imagine it, thinking about all kinds of things. How we would have shared everything together. How we would have read books together, done our homework together, gossiped together, shared little secrets together. How we would have laughed with the Flanagan boys every Sunday night at Ipanema Restaurant. How we would have memorized every single *Perry Mason* episode, and dreamed about a mom like Annie Oakley, and eaten bags and bags of M&Ms.

I thought about how my little sister might have come along when I was thirteen, leaving for Milan to jump-start my modeling career. How we might have gone to Café Zucca together, or "shopped 'til we dropped" in the Quadrilatero, or seen *Aida* at La

Scala, or visited the Duomo, or stared at *The Last Supper,* or dined on *saffron risotto* at Cracco's with the champ.

Within these conjurings, all these wonderful fantasies, as I stared down at my dead sister, my fantasized sister never actually had a name.

What *was* her name?

Was it Irina?

Was it Lisa Livingston?

Was it something else?

Lisa Livingston, it seemed, had absolutely no record of any kind. No paper trail. No data trail. No past. No history. Even her fingerprints had turned up nothing in the databases. All that I knew about my dead little sister, the only thing that distinguished her in any way, was that neat little tattoo on her right breast.

BHC

Aside from that, she was blank.

Nothing.

At least she didn't seem to have a criminal record, even though it was now perfectly clear that she'd killed Mitchell Carlyle, snuggling up to the smitten cadet and blowing a .38 through his brain.

"There's no residue on her hand, Deirdre," the captain had questioned skeptically on the day after the Times Square killings.

"Because she fired the gun with her glove on," I explained. "Then she tossed it off the edge of the roof, just before she was pushed off herself."

"That's a lot of ifs."

"No woman," I insisted, "wearing a Donna Karan evening gown would *ever* lose one of those gloves."

The captain shrugged, but he wasn't shrugging me off, it was just one of his "What do I know?" shrugs.

Later, of course, Carlos had retrieved the glove from the Barton Building.

But *why* had my sister killed the young cadet in cold blood? What in the world could have induced her to do such a thing?

Her aunt?

"Margarita"?

Ever since I'd first encountered "Margarita" on the terrace at the DK showroom, I'd believed that the woman was behind everything that was happening.

But why?

Was she really Irina's aunt?

If she was, that meant that "Margarita," whoever she was, was the sister of whoever-it-was that the champ had slept with nearly two decades ago. The sister of the woman who'd given birth to Irina.

I pushed it from my mind, but my mind kept racing.

Who was "Margarita"?
What was her real name?
Had she manipulated Irina into killing Mitchell Carlyle?
Had she pushed Irina off the top of Times Square One?
Had she sent an assassin to kill Jason Parker at the Unisphere?
Had she orchestrated the assassination of a US senator?
Had she sent an assassin to kill me?

Why?

How was it possible that someone could be filled with so much vitriol?

So much hatred?

Maybe I was wrong.

Maybe "Margarita" was just a cog in the wheel of whatever was going on. Or maybe she was just some innocent woman who'd used a stolen credit card to buy a pretty dress for her niece. Maybe she was just someone who was delighted that her niece had fallen in love with a handsome cadet from West Point.

I didn't know.

But now, of course, things had gotten much worse.

Uncle Pat didn't come home last night.

He was missing.

Maybe kidnapped.

Maybe dead.

I tried to push such terrifying thoughts from my mind. My uncle had always seemed indestructible, and I was counting on that fact. I was relying on it.

For now, my job was to keep my head on straight and try and figure things out.

Which always came back to "Margarita."

Overwhelmed, I stared down at Irina, and I gently placed my hand over the dead hand of my little sister. It was coldish, stiffish, lifeless, but she was still my little sister. I'd grown up in a house, in a gym, of tough-guy macho men, never crying very much, but I did right now. I let myself feel everything—the depthless longing, the loss, the lost love—and I cried.

I also felt something else. Something that I'd never felt before. A craving for vengeance. I knew that it was wrong, and I knew that it was always invariably unproductive, but I couldn't deny how I felt. Somebody had killed my sister, and somebody had done something to my uncle, and somebody was going to pay for it.

I leaned over my sister and kissed her on the forehead.

With love.

20. Gapstow Bridge

I WAS SITTING IN my favorite seat.

It was another beautiful afternoon in the park.

I was watching the ducks float across the peaceful surface of the Pond, but I was also alert, with my Glock ready and waiting in my Louis Vuitton tote. In a way, I was almost hoping that somebody would come after me today. I had a lot of anger that I needed to expiate.

To distract myself, I looked down at my M&Ms, laid out in their usual fashion, but it was no use. Even such an always-reliable pleasure was denied to me at the moment, so I put the reds and blues and greens and the rest of them back into my little container, then dropped them back into my tote.

Maybe later.

Maybe after I'd talked to my old man.

"There's something you need to understand about your father," the captain had once told me when I was about ten years old. "He's too kind. *Much* too kind. Way too generous."

My uncle gave me a moment to let it sink in, then he tried to explain.

"Your father's the best friend that I've ever had. Much more than just a brother. But he's way too trusting. Way too easygoing."

I pointed to the empty boxing ring.

Ring Number Two.

My uncle and I were sitting in the empty gym that night while the champ was out to dinner with one of his pugilistic protégés. It was exactly two days after Carlos, who was only fourteen at the time, had discovered that one of the other trainers had been embezzling money from the gym.

Since the captain always understood me, he knew exactly why I was pointing at the boxing ring.

"You're right, Sweetheart. Your dad was *never* easygoing in the ring. He was always a hard-hard worker, very focused, with serious goals. That was true whenever he was fighting, and it's still true whenever he's training the young kids. But as for the rest of his life, he's much too trusting. He's the kind of man that people take advantage of."

Even though I was only ten years old at the time, I understood what my uncle was *really* trying to say. Without actually saying it. He was letting me know that my old man was a bit of a sucker. An easy mark. And even then, at the age of ten, I knew it was true. I'd seen the old fighters stop by for a pair of fifties. Even when they really didn't need it. I'd watched my father giving everything—his time, his love, his equipment—to all kinds of punky kids who didn't deserve it. Who later turned against him.

"But isn't it good to be good?" I asked my uncle.

"Sure," the captain assured me. "I wish I was half the man your father is. But you and I have to watch out for him. We can't let people take advantage of him."

I nodded.

I understood.

Over the next nine years, the captain and Carlos and I had done our best to protect the champ from himself. But now it seemed that the man who was "so good" had been deceiving me my entire life, and it was time to find out why. Naturally, there was a part of me that was extremely angry that I'd never known I'd had a sister, but there was another part of me that kept saying, over and over, "Just give the champ a chance. Give him a chance to explain himself."

Which is exactly what I planned to do.

It was almost time.

I saw Carlos waving from the southwest end of the bridge. He looked rather pleased, and I was certain he'd found a useful photograph.

"How fortunate I am," I thought to myself, "to have Carlos in my life."

In my family.

Carlos approached the bench, looking around cautiously.

"It's all right," I assured him, "I've been watching carefully. Watching *everything*."

"Well, don't tell your uncle," Carlos said, and I agreed, appreciating the fact that Carlos believed the captain was still alive. That he'd pop up soon. Any minute. That he'd be mad as hell that Carlos had left me alone in the park for thirty minutes.

But I'd convinced him.

"If they're really still after me," I reasoned, "I want to keep them away from the gym until we've got the photo."

As always, I was trying to protect the old man, which Carlos understood.

"Besides, I need some time to think. Don't worry, I'll be out in the open with my Glock right beside me."

Finally, Carlos had relented, dropping me off at the park before he drove down to the photographer's studio.

"Here it is," he said, removing two eight-by-tens from a manila envelope.

The first was a wide shot of the crowded, glittering floor of the Waldorf Ballroom, taken on the night of the Sweethearts' Ball. The photographer had been hired by the NYC chapter of the American Heart Association, and Carlos had tracked him down.

"Her box is up in the left-hand corner," he pointed out.

Yes.

There she was.

"Margarita."

Sitting all alone in a stunning yellow dress, sleek, strapless, probably Armani.

She was looking down at the ballroom floor.

"Now check out the blowup."

I looked at the second eight-by-ten. It was a blowup of the left-hand corner of the wider shot.

There she was again. Looking absolutely radiant. Looking voluptuous. Her beautiful face was a tiny bit soft, but the overall blowup wasn't blurry at all. As a matter of fact, it was remarkably clear and sharp.

"Not bad," Carlos said.

"Excellent," I agreed.

I looked up at Carlos.

"You're the best, Carlos."

I meant it, but as he always did with compliments, he pretended that he didn't hear it.

I put the pictures away and collected myself.

It was time to talk to the old man.

21. Carmelita

I WALKED THROUGH the busy gym, into my father's office, and shut the door.

"Anything?" I asked.

"Nothing. I just checked with Dempsey."

The champ was worried in a way that I'd never seen him worry before, but I understood. After all, who was more important to the both of us than Uncle Pat?

The old man swung his wheelchair around to face me, trying to put a good face on the situation.

"He'll turn up, Sweetheart. He's the toughest guy on the planet. He'll be all right."

I wanted to agree, but I couldn't, so I answered another way.

"Carlos'll find him."

Which left unsaid whether I expected my uncle to be found dead or alive.

"Yeah," the champ agreed. "I just heard Carlos parking his Trans Am. He's back in his office."

Which I already knew.

Now it was time to get down to business.

"We need to talk."

The old man could see that I was serious, and he naturally assumed it was about Uncle Pat's disappearance.

"About your past," I clarified.

Since he had no idea what I was talking about, he waited patiently as I pulled up a chair and sat down in front of him. I opened the manila envelope, pulled out the second eight-by-ten, and handed it to my father.

"I need to know who this is."

My old man looked at the woman in the color photograph, and his whole world seemed to implode. He looked desperate, even pathetic. I'd never seen him like this before. Then he placed the photograph in his lap, and he stared at me with a terrible and shameful resignation.

"I did it to protect you, Deirdre."

I had no doubt about that, but I needed straight answers.

"Who is she?"

He hesitated.

He stared into my eyes.

"Who is she?" I repeated.

"Your mother."

It was mid-June in New York City.

The gym, as always, was hotter than hell, but I went instantly frigid, as cold as my little sister lying in the morgue. I felt terribly alone. Even with my father sitting right in front of me. Even within his normally comforting presence. I felt cut off from everyone and everything. Abandoned. I felt a kind of loneliness that had never been a part of my life before. It seemed as though there was a kind of invasive malignancy surrounding me. Surrounding my entire life.

I fought against it, with all my will, with all my strength, and somehow, I managed to keep myself calm.

At least on the outside.

"Who's the woman in the photograph upstairs?" I heard myself ask, referring to the picture of "my mother" on the wall of my bedroom. The one that I spoke to every day, that I prayed for, that I prayed to.

"It's an old shot of Rexana," the champ admitted.

Honestly, shamefully.

I hardly noticed.

I was now, I knew, in some kind of shock. Shocked by the simple fact that the woman who called herself "Margarita" was actually my mother. Shocked by the extent of my father's pernicious lie. A lifetime lie.

A lifetime of deception.

"Forgive me," he said, weakly, desperately.

As if in a daze, as if guided by a lifetime of nothing but love for the broken man sitting in front of me, I leaned forward and kissed his forehead.

Then I sat back in my chair.

"Tell me everything."

"I will."

Which he did.

Doing so in such a way that I was certain there was no further deception. Aware that, in the very act of his telling the truth, he was experiencing a tangible visceral relief that the deception was finally over.

No matter how difficult it was for the both of us.

Her real name was Carmelita.

Carmelita Rivera.

She'd exploded into the champ's already wild life at the MGM Grand in Vegas after his second title defense against Auturo Ruiz. That night, the champ had mercilessly battered Ruiz from post to post for three excruciating rounds before the ref put an end to it. After the fight, after the press conference, everyone in the champ's corner, high on victory, celebrated at a private party at the casino. Then Carmelita popped up from nowhere. The old man had no idea who she was, or where she came from, but he didn't care. She was flashy, voluptuous, charming, and dressed to kill in a slinky red dress. If there was a definitive knockout that night, it happened when the champ got his first glimpse of Carmelita Rivera.

Suddenly, nothing else mattered in his life.

Who could care about something as insignificant as a world championship belt, or anything else, when a woman like Carmelita walked into your life?

The next day, when the captain, who wasn't a captain yet, along with the rest of the champ's small entourage, returned to Manhattan, the champ stayed in Vegas. It was a maelstrom. A whirlwind. A blur. A kaleidoscope.

They were married the next day.

Two days after the fight.

She'd been born, so she said, in Santa Marta, Columbia. She'd come to the United States when she was fifteen years old. She loved the ocean, and she was eager to improve herself. She claimed that she'd been emotionally abused by her mother, but that was all behind her now. She was working in public relations for a firm in Manhattan, and she was, supposedly, living on East Sixty-Second.

The day after the wedding, the champ woke up in his empty bed at the MGM Grand and discovered that Carmelita was gone. He also discovered that she'd taken the ten thousand dollars in cash that the champ had pulled from his bank account for their proposed honeymoon in Waikiki. Like a deranged desperate fool in some kind of old film noir, the champ relentlessly searched for Carmelita for two days and two nights, roaming, all alone, from casino to casino. Finally, he gave up, flew back to New York, and confessed everything to his older brother, who tried to track her down, but came up with nothing.

He paused.

It was a tough story to tell, even for a tough guy.

The angry part of me wanted to say, "So I was conceived in a Las Vegas hotel room with a woman you barely knew?"

But I didn't.

"Go ahead, dad," I encouraged gently, "tell me the rest."

He did.

Back in Manhattan, the champ tried to deal with the anxiety and the shame in the only way he knew how. With the sweet science. For the next six months, he trained like a maniac for his next fight, a non-title bout in the Garden with the new IBF Middleweight Champ, an ex-con from Philly named Bernard Hopkins. But the old man overtrained, and his head wasn't in the right place. He was walking into the ring against a guy who was kicking off a Hall of Fame career, and Hopkins took him apart in the Garden that night, knocking him senseless in the third round. It was the champ's first professional loss, and it was the first time that he'd ever been knocked out. It was the first time that he'd ever been knocked off his feet. It was devastating, but he still had the title, and he was still young. He still had time to get his life and his career back on track.

A month later, the accident happened.

Of course, this part of the story I already knew, but not in the context of what was really going on in my father's life. It happened late one night when the champ was hanging at Jimmy's Corner with my uncle, who got a hot tip about an ongoing drug case. Before heading home, they stopped at some rundown three-story near Tenth Avenue. While my uncle went up on the roof to meet his snitch, the champ waited in the cab. When a gunshot went off, my old man raced inside the building, rushing to the rooftop, but it was empty. Everything was silent. Wondering if his brother was back downstairs, the champ walked over to the edge of the roof to look at the street below. At that exact moment, he was shot in the back of the thigh by some coked-out ex-con. Losing his balance, he fell off the roof, breaking his lower back and ending up in a wheelchair.

Then things got worse.

Two months later, out of the blue, Carmelita called the champ on the phone and told him there was a baby. She explained what she wanted, and the old man agreed, but he didn't tell his brother. Two days later, some sketchy go-between arrived at the gym, dropped off the baby, and picked up the payment.

"How much?" I asked.

After all, who wouldn't be curious to know how much her mother had sold her for?

"Does it matter?" he asked wearily.

"I don't know."

The champ thought it over. He wanted to come clean about everything.

Complete disclosure.

"A million."

Which was probably everything the champ had at the time. If not more. Sure, the champ was a "champ," but he was a champ in a low-visibility boxing division. Super-middle. Sure, he was extremely popular in the city, like all Irish fighters, but he was just beginning to build his reputation elsewhere. He was, in fact, on the cusp of getting big-time pay-per-view coverage when Bernard Hopkins turned his lights out. Then he ended up retired in a wheelchair.

"Did you have to borrow?" I asked.

"Yes."

"Did Uncle Pat know?"

"Not until it was over."

He looked at me.

"All I wanted was my baby girl."

I wanted to cry, but I didn't.

I reached out my hand and placed it gently over his. He was trembling, something I'd never seen before. I wanted to put an end to it. I wanted to say, "Dad, we can finish this some other time," but of course, I couldn't. At least seven people were already dead, another had been shot, and another was missing. I was still in danger, and so was my father.

I needed to know *everything*, and I needed to know it right now.

"Tell me the rest."

The next day, the champ, sitting in his wheelchair and holding a two-week-old baby, told his brother the truth. Uncle Pat didn't say much. He didn't even reprimand his younger brother for being an idiot. Instead, he listened carefully.

Then he said:

"I'll find that bitch."

The Flanagan brothers, as was well known at the precinct and within the boxing world, were notorious non-swearers, the result of yet another vow they'd taken a few months after the Guinness vow. But "bitch," "bastard," "damn," and "hell," had all been deemed acceptable, for emphasis, for special occasions.

Then the captain went after Carmelita, tracking her down in Mexico, but she was dead. She'd drowned in a water-skiing accident off Acapulco.

"She always loved the ocean," the champ repeated.

Oddly enough, he took her death hard. *Very* hard. Despite everything that she'd done, the champ was still, naively, hoping for something better. To him, she seemed a magically charming, capable person, and he'd been fantasizing about a future in which Carmelita would turn her life around and come back to him.

The captain, of course, had *no* patience for that kind of thinking, perfectly content that the little "bitch" was out of his brother's life. Besides, the champ now had a little baby to take care of.

"I didn't want you to know," the old man tried to explain, "that you had a mother like that. I also didn't want you to know what a fool I'd been."

He thought it over, then looked into my eyes.

"But it was the best thing that ever happened in my life. It brought you into my life, Sweetheart, and you *are* my life."

He wasn't finished.

"Believe me, it's the *only* secret, Deirdre. I promise."

I believed him.

I also knew that I had no right to be too self-righteous about *his* secret, given that I had a secret of my own.

Now it was time for some more truths.

"Carmelita's still alive."

"That's impossible."

"I've met her."

He was stunned.

Painfully stunned.

"But Pat told me she was dead."

"Then he lied," I assured him. "Or he made up the drowning to make you forget her. I'm not sure which."

"I can't believe it."

"It's true."

His brother had deceived him, as they'd deceived me.

The champ was having trouble processing everything, but I needed to move forward. I told him about "Margarita" and what I knew about her involvement in the case. He listened in silence, in bewilderment, then wondered out loud.

"Is that why my brother's missing?"

"I don't know."

"It's all my fault."

"It's all *her* fault."

The champ nodded, like a man who feels guilty about everything.

But it wasn't over yet.

It was time to tell him about the pretty young girl who'd fallen to her death in Times Square.

"There's more, dad."

He waited.

"I have a sister."

22. Bryant Park

I WAS SITTING ON top of seven million books in the most densely occupied park in the world. I was also, carefully, watching everyone around me, with my Glock 19 ready and waiting in my open tote. At the other end of Bryant Park, on Fifth Avenue, Carlos was somewhere inside the New York Public Library, trying to figure out how everything tied together, especially the connection between Carmelita and Senator Carlyle.

I'd already figured out part of the answer, sitting here in the twilight, running the letters through my mind, over and over again:

BHC

Or maybe:

BHCE

Two days ago, the Coroner's Office had called Dempsey about the little tattoo on Irina's right breast. As best he could ascertain, the coroner believed that the fourth letter, which had been intentionally removed, was "E."

Which still led Dempsey nowhere:

> *Behavioral Health Consulting Experts*
> *The Bureau of Higher and Continuing Education*
> *The Bureau of Health Care Eligibility*
> *Breast Health & Cancer Education*
> *The* Ben-Hur *Collector's Edition*

So I was sitting in the park thinking things over, watching the office workers cutting through the park on their way home from work, past the tai chi ladies, the chess players, and the off-key folkies with their guitars. Not to mention the hundreds of summer relaxers enjoying the fading twilight in the heart of the greatest city in the world.

But what if it wasn't an "E"?

What if it was an "F"?

That made things easy.

Bedford Hills Correctional Facility

Bedford Hills, Westchester County, was the largest women's prison in New York State. It was also the state's only maximum-security prison for women.

As sad as it was to speculate, it seemed possible that my sister, "Lisa" or "Irina" (whoever she was), had done some time at Bedford Hills. Which really didn't make sense since she didn't have a data trail, either from fingerprints or DNA. Besides, why would someone scar herself with the initials of such a horrible place on one of her breasts? I couldn't fathom an answer, but I could certainly understand why she'd eventually had one of the letters removed.

After all, every cop in the state would recognize the initials "BHCF."

Maybe it also explained the connection with Senator Carlyle. Before he ran for political office, Alan Carlyle had been a federal prosecutor.

Maybe he'd put Irina in Bedford Hills.

Something like that.

Whatever the case, I was getting closer, and I knew it, and I was certain that when Carlos came out of the library, probably the greatest library in the world, he'd know everything that we needed to know.

In the meantime, I did my best to relax, which wasn't too difficult. I've always loved Bryant Park, a little green oasis in the middle of the hectic garment district, named for the great poet who'd written two of the many poems that I'd studied and memorized and loved in high school: "To a Waterfowl" and "Thanatopsis."

> *Thou go not, like the quarry-slave at night,*
> *Scourged to his dungeon, but sustained and soothed*
> *By an unfaltering trust, approach thy grave,*
> *Like one who wraps the drapery of his couch*
> *About him, and lies down to pleasant dreams.*

Back in the 1840s, William Cullen Bryant, editor of the *New York Evening Post*, had been the first person to publicly demand a "central park" for his rapidly expanding city. His wish, of course, eventually came to fruition with Olmsted's construction of Central Park. Then ten years after the poet's death, the city, ironically, renamed this little park, built on the site of an old potter's field, as "Bryant Park."

Unfortunately, by the 1970s, the loveliest place in the city south of Central Park had deteriorated into a drug-infested, crime-infested "Needle Park," but a carefully planned yet still miraculous restoration brought the park back to life in the 1990s. Eventually, it had a Café, a Grill, Le Carrousel, an ice rink in the winter, a film festival, a concert series, and amazingly enough, every February and September, it was also the site of the famous "Seventh on Sixth" Fashion Show, the only event in Bryant Park not opened to the public.

Later, the fashion show was moved to Lincoln Center, but I'll never forget the incredible excitement of my first New York City runway, right here in Bryant Park. I was only twelve years old, very impressionable, and there was a lot to be impressed about. I remember the first time I spotted Anna Wintour, sitting in the first row with a bunch of celebrities, including Bono and Nicole Kidman.

Of course, what I remember the most is the stunning white dress that I wore for Oscar de la Renta, the one I *never* wanted to take off. I also remember the heavenly foods from Dean and Deluca, and sneaking a glass of Möet champagne when the old man wasn't looking. Best of all, I remember making so many new friends that day, including girls from all the other agencies like Wilhelmina, Elite, and IMG.

Tonight, I was watching an endless variety of New Yorkers walking by, wearing "ordinary" clothes, and I enjoyed it immensely. I've never grown tired of people-watching in the city I love so much, but now, I was keeping myself alert, watching for anyone who might be watching for me, planning to murder me in Bryant Park.

Or anywhere else.

So I kept an eye on everyone, looking over the darkening grass that stretched before me, fully aware of the rather bizarre fact that *right beneath me*, under the lawn, which was the largest stretch of grass south of Central Park, there were over seven million books.

Stored in unseen underground vaults.

Then I spotted Carlos.

There were probably two thousand people walking, sitting, or milling about the park tonight, but Carlos, in his own shy and self-effacing way, stood out from everyone. He wore, as he almost always did, wrangler jeans with a dark buttoned-down dress shirt. His shirts might be blue, or burgundy, or black, but they were *always* dark. He always looked, at least, to me, like some kind of a movie star.

As he got closer, I could tell from the look on his face that he knew everything we needed to know.

As usual, Carlos held a little stack of index cards in his right hand, neatly bound with a red rubber band. He might be a computer whiz, but his note-taking was decidedly old school.

Without a word, he sat down beside me and began to summarize.

Without a wasted word.

Seventeen years ago, Carmelita Rivera Flanagan had been convicted at the Albany courthouse of murdering her own mother and was subsequently sentenced to twenty-four years without parole.

"Her mother?" I repeated, almost reflexively.

Meaning my grandmother.

Maybe I shouldn't have been shocked, but I was.

"Yeah, her mother."

Even though I could probably figure out the rest of it, I wanted to hear all the facts from Carlos:

Alan Carlyle had prosecuted the case, and the captain had been a witness for the prosecution.

"He must have cut a deal to keep the champ out of it," Carlos speculated as I nodded in agreement.

"But how'd she get out of Bedford Hills?" I wondered.

He didn't bother to ask how I knew it was Bedford Hills.

"It's a little vague," he admitted, "but everything looks legal. She got out about three months ago."

"She certainly didn't waste any time," I said, as if to myself.

Carlos nodded.

"There's something else, Deirdre."

I waited.

"In her second year at Bedford Hills, she had a child."

I was astonished. Heartsick. I hadn't done the math. I'd foolishly assumed that Carmelita had given birth to my sister *before* she'd gone to prison.

"A daughter?"

"Yes."

"Irina?"

"Yes."

"So my little sister was born in a prison?"

"Yes."

We sat there, together, probably looking perfectly anonymous, looking like everyone else in the park, within the falling shadows of the fading sunset, thinking about the staggering vindictiveness of Carmelita Rivera. Thinking about her obsessiveness. Thinking about how she must have sat in her cell in Bedford Hills, fermenting within a tempestuous maelstrom of rage, of hatred.

Planning her revenge.

On everyone.

"You're next," Carlos said calmly.

"Maybe," I said, not disagreeing. "Who was Carmelita's defense attorney back then?"

"A guy named Keith Palmero."

I nodded again.

I was worrying about the champ. I'm sure that Carlos was worrying as well.

Maybe my father was next.

I posed an obvious question, a rhetorical question, one that could never be answered.

"What kind of woman kills her own mother?"

23. Flanagan's Gym

S HAKIRA WAS at it again.

Carmelita might be out there somewhere, plotting who-knows-what, but I still needed my daily workout.

"Whenever, Wherever" was blasting through the gym speakers for the second time this morning, as Eddie Mays and his younger brother Tommy worked the double Dutch ropes with rhythmic precision with me in the midst, frenetically doing my best to defy gravity within the whirling nylon ropes, soaked with sweat.

My cell rang.

Usually, I never take my phone into the gym. They're actually banned by the champ, but now, everything had changed.

I finished, grabbed a small towel, and slumped down to the floor, against the wall, within the yellow-marked confines of Deirdre's Corner.

I answered the phone.

Breathlessly.

It wasn't, as I'd hoped, about my uncle.

In the meantime, the Mays brothers had hung up my skipping ropes and gone back to their prework workouts. Then Carlos came out of his office, which was really a large closet in the back of the gym, walked over to Deirdre's Corner, and sat down beside me.

My conversation with Dempsey was short and sweet, and I hung up the phone and looked at Carlos.

"Keith Palmero is dead."

"I know."

"Dempsey," I continued anyway, "says that Palmero was shot in his car last week, outside his home in Albany."

Carlos nodded.

"I guess he didn't do a good enough job at the trial."

I wiped away the sweat that was streaming down my face.

"Anything new on Uncle Pat?"

"Not yet. I'm working on it."

Of course he was, and I was sorry that I'd brought it up.

He continued.

"Carmelita's been a very busy ex-con."

"Tell me."

"She got married again."

I was amazed.

Again and again, I found myself astonished by this clearly deranged woman who was supposed to be my mother.

"She's now Carmelita Walker. Carmelita Rivera Flanagan Walker. Her husband was a retired investment banker living at the Jersey Shore."

"Was?"

"Yeah, he's dead too. She met him two months ago, and they got married a week later. Three weeks after that, the old guy had an 'accident,' drowning off Brigantine Beach."

"How much was he worth?"

"Tons."

"Naturally," I said uselessly.

Carmelita was trouble enough without money, and now she's got "tons."

"I'm going to Brigantine," I decided.

"I know. I'll drive you down."

I shook my head.

"I'll get Dempsey. I want you here. Finding the captain and protecting the old man."

He understood.

Even though he didn't like me going off without him, he trusted Dempsey.

Implicitly.

"All right."

I looked at Carlos. He was wearing a black T-shirt with "Flanagan's Gym" printed across the front in white letters.

"Where's your piece?"

"It's in my office."

We all knew that Carlos didn't care much for guns, which is why the captain bought him a Glock 19 five years ago. He learned how to use it, and he accepted the fact that there were times when it was necessary.

"I'd like you carrying," I said.

"In the gym?"

"Yeah, use your shoulder harness and a baggy sweatshirt."

I thought back to the frenzy at the Storm King Cabins.

"Luis Salazar won't waste any time," I added.

He understood.

"No problem."

"I'd like to talk to everyone in the gym before the champ comes down."

As always, Carlos understood.

We stood up together, then walked over to Ring Number One. As I slipped through the ropes onto the canvas floor of the ring, Carlos banged the "round" bell three times, and everyone in the gym stopped and looked at me, which despite the old man's Rule Number Fourteen, seemed perfectly acceptable.

There were about forty guys in the gym, all of whom were deadly serious about the sport. Most of them were in their late teens or early twenties. Most of them were from poor and often dysfunctional homes. Most of them were from the worst parts of the city. *All* of them were "tough guys," but none of them were punks or creeps. Carlos had made sure of that. They were all good kids. Good young men.

"Miss Flanagan," Carlos called to his boxers, "would like a word."

I stepped to the edge of the ring and looked over the top rope.

"I think you all know that the captain is missing, and some of you are probably also aware that the champ is in danger. Later today, they're sending somebody from Midtown South to hang at the gym, and somebody'll be here twenty-four seven, but I'd still like all of you to be alert."

I hesitated.

The words caught in my throat. I was just as surprised as everyone else in the gym, but somehow, I fought through my welling emotions.

"You know how much the champ loves all you guys . . ."

I faltered again, then quickly managed to collect myself and finish.

"Please, keep him safe. *Please.*"

Carlos spread the top two ropes, and I slipped out of the ring and went back upstairs to my apartment.

24. Brigantine

I S IT WRONG to love a place like Atlantic City?
    If it is, I can't help it.

As Dempsey and I headed toward the casino skyline, toward the Atlantic Ocean, I remembered all the wonderful times I'd had at the Summer Fashion Shows at Caesars, beginning when I was thirteen years old. I especially remembered spoiling myself on the last day of every show (with the champ's permission) at Spa Toccare at the Borgata.

I also had fond memories of the ISSF Junior Pistol Championships, where I'd come away with two firsts and a third.

But what I remembered most fondly about Atlantic City was when Gina, Mary Lou, Elissa, and I competed in the Girls' Metro Team Skipping Championships when I was fifteen years old. It was a combination of both individual and double Dutch skipping, and we gave it everything we had, coming in second to Missy Mays's amazing gang of girls from the South Bronx. The following year, we were back again, even more prepared, even more determined, and we still came in second. Again. Finally, in my senior year at St. Dominic's, we came back for our last chance and won it all, and all those earlier near-misses made the final victory even sweeter.

Of course, in another and much better world, Irina would have been skipping on the team alongside me.

Dempsey turned north, taking the bridge to Brigantine, a sleepy, friendly, high-property-value beach town on Brigantine Beach Island, just north of Atlantic City. During one of my modeling trips at Caesars, I'd spent a free morning roaming the Wildlife Refuge at the north end of the island, and a free afternoon on Brigantine's lovely six-mile beach, often staring off the coast, trying to imagine the three hundred or so ships that had been shipwrecked off the coast on the Brigantine shoals.

But Henry Hudson's *Half Moon* never wrecked out there. Neither did the swift privateer, captained by the notorious William Kidd of Greenock, Scotland, who buried a locked and heavy chest on the Brigantine coast in 1698, along with, so it's reported, the fresh remains of the only other man who knew the exact burial spot—Timothy Jones, who was Kidd's first mate. According to legend, Kidd had fallen in love with a local Brigantine girl named Amanda before he was eventually captured near Boston and shipped back to England, where he was hanged in 1701.

So it was right here, on this pretty island, with its fascinating history, its lighthouse, its seawall, its stunning sunsets, its violent storms, and its unforgettable views of the Atlantic City skyline, where Carmelita Rivera had finally ended up. At least, for a little while, since Dempsey and I naturally assumed that, by now, she was long gone.

Dempsey turned right off Ocean Avenue, heading south on Twenty-Eighth Street toward the Atlantic. Then he slowed down and pulled over.

"It's the one on the right," he said, pointing at the Walker house.

It was hardly a beach "cottage."

It was huge.

It was darkish, mostly wooden, with colorful gardens, looking a bit like a well-kept Spanish hacienda. Around the back, there was a tremendous swimming pool, which seemed rather superfluous since the house was sitting right on the beach. It was also fenced and gated, but the most intriguing thing about the Walker house, from my point of view, was the little red sign on the front gate.

"Sold."

"She's gone," I said, realizing that I'd been hoping for the impossible.

"Maybe," Dempsey said, "but I still want to take a look around."

He turned sideways in the front seat to face me.

"You stay right here, Deirdre. Keep your eyes open."

He meant it, so I agreed.

"Where's your popgun?"

I removed the Glock from my Prada handbag and laid it in my lap.

"I'll be fine."

Dempsey was still worried.

"I'm fine," I repeated.

Reluctantly, Dempsey nodded, got out of the unmarked cruiser, walked through the front gate, which was open, and knocked on the front door. When there was no response, he walked around the back of the house, which also looked vacant.

As soon as Dempsey was out of sight, the front door opened, and a large, imposing man in a blue business suit exited quietly through the front door. He walked to the gate and stepped to the sidewalk. He was carrying a large stack of folders under his left arm, and he was heading in my direction. When he saw me sitting in the car, he immediately cut across the street and walked up the driveway of a seemingly deserted beach cottage.

I could hear Dempsey's voice repeating inside my head, over and over, "You stay right here," but I couldn't do it. I couldn't just sit here in the stupid car and let the guy walk away with whatever he was carrying. I grabbed my weapon, got out of the cruiser, and followed the huge man in the blue suit.

Cautiously, quickly, I rushed around the left side of the house across the street and waited. The backyard was empty, and no one seemed to be inside the house.

Everything was silent.

Where was the huge man?

I waited, trying to be patient, with the Glock in my hand and my heart racing.

Nothing happened.

Maybe he went inside the house?

Slowly, I moved along the backside of the house, looking into the windows as I went. All was still. Then I heard a faint noise from around the corner. Finally, fed up, I stepped around the corner and saw the large man bent over, kneeling on the ground in front of me. As he straightened up, still on his knees, I put the Glock in his face.

"Don't use that thing!" he called out.

He was terrified.

He also didn't seem to be carrying.

"I just wanted some pictures!" he explained. "That's all! Nothing else!"

I glanced down at the ground. It was covered with family pictures. Color shots and black and whites. The man must have dropped one of his files.

"I'm with NYPD," I said firmly, trying to reassure the man, but still keeping my weapon ready.

He didn't believe me.

Fortunately, Dempsey rushed up the driveway, flashed his badge, and took charge, asking:

"What were you doing in the house across the street?"

"It's my father's house. I just wanted to get some family pictures."

Dempsey understood.

"You're David Walker?"

"Yes."

David Walker, as we both knew, was the son of Ethan Walker, the man who'd married Carmelita before ending up dead three weeks later.

"Pick up your stuff," Dempsey said. "We need to talk."

The man retrieved the rest of his pictures as Dempsey gave me a look that said, without actually saying it, "I thought I told you to stay in the cruiser."

A few minutes later, I was sitting on a comfortable couch in the recently sold Walker beach house staring out at the Atlantic Ocean. Dempsey was checking out the house, and Walker was sitting wearily in a nearby chair. He was a local lawyer who worked for one of the casinos. Dempsey had already checked him out, and the guy was clean, just like his old man. He was about thirty-five and unmarried, and he'd lived with his father until Carmelita came along. Right now, the poor guy looked frightened, even with Dempsey in the house, and I felt bad that I'd been so aggressive across the street.

"I'm sorry," I said.

He nodded.

"You know something?" he reflected. "I'd never actually seen a gun before until that woman came into our lives."

I understood.

Dempsey reentered the living room and didn't waste time.

"Tell me about your father."

"My father married a psychopath," Walker said with a shrug, as if that explained everything.

Dempsey waited.

"My mom died about five years ago, and my dad took it hard. *Very* hard. He'd been a banker, and he'd retired early, and he was lonely. Lonely and vulnerable. Then the bitch came along, and that was that. They were married in no time."

He snapped his fingers.

"Then my father was dead."

"Did she do it?" Dempsey asked.

"Of course she did it, but I've got no proof, and besides, she's not somebody I want to mess around with."

"Did she ever use any other names?"

"No, just Carmelita Rivera."

"Do you know where she is?"

"No."

"How did they meet?" I wondered.

"At a fundraiser."

Which sounded familiar.

"When did you see her last?" Dempsey continued.

"About three weeks ago. Just before she sold the house."

Once again, Walker got visibly nervous.

"Look, all I wanted was some old pictures of my mom and my dad. So I snuck back in here before she sold the furniture. I grew up in this house, but she took it away, and she also took all his money. She even arranged to cut me out of his will, but I've still got a trust fund she doesn't know about, and all I want to do is put this nightmare behind me."

"Have you been threatened?" Dempsey asked.

He laughed.

"In no uncertain terms. She's got this pair of crazy Dominican thugs who do anything she wants. I'm sure they drowned my father."

Walker was a man who wasn't ashamed to admit his fears, and I couldn't blame him.

"Did she ever mention," I wondered, "any places that she liked to visit?"

"Well, she's a 'beacher.' That's for sure! She loves to water-ski."

"Did they have a honeymoon?"

"Of course! Guess who picked it? They cruised around the Caribbean for three weeks. Antigua, Barbados, St. Vincent, and several other islands. My father told me that the bitch loved it, especially Barbados."

He grew pensive.

"You know," he said vaguely, "I've never met one before."

"Met what?"

"A psychopath. I mean you see them in the movies all the time, and you hear about them on the news, but you never expect one of them to come into your family and kill your father."

He looked at me directly, sadly.

"All I want to do is leave this place. I'm getting the hell out of here. *Far* away."

"I need to know where you're going," Dempsey pointed out.

He was reluctant.

"Is it necessary?"

"You can trust me," Dempsey assured him.

Walker took out one of his business cards and wrote an address on the back. It was some place in New Mexico.

My cell phone rang.

It was Carlos, and my heart sank.

I also knew something about fear.

"Carlos?"

"Yeah," he said, wasting no time, "I've found him."

"Is he alive?"

25. Presbyterian Hospital

WHEN DEMPSEY DROPPED ME off in front of the hospital on Sixty-Ninth, Carlos was waiting outside.

"Is he still conscious?" I asked, as we rushed inside.

"Yes, and he's asking for you."

We were waiting at the elevator.

"How is he?"

"Not bad, considering."

"Considering" that he'd been shot point-blank in the back, had all his IDs stolen, and was taken to Presbyterian, where he'd been lying unconscious and unidentified for nearly twenty-four hours.

The irony was infuriating. The captain of Midtown South ends up unrecognized on Sixty-Ninth Street.

"Who shot him?"

"He doesn't know, but somebody took his wallet, his badge, and his weapon."

"A mugging?"

"Maybe. He doesn't remember the gunshot."

Meaning that he'd probably been shot with a suppressor.

By Luis Salazar.

"Where?"

"On Forty-Fourth, near Jimmy's."

As the elevator rose, I tried not to think about it. Instead, I looked at Carlos.

"Thanks for everything."

I meant it, and Carlos *knew* I meant it, but he still wasn't pleased with himself.

"I should have found him sooner," he said, almost to himself. "He woke up two hours after I tracked him down, so we would have found him tonight anyway."

"I'm sure he was glad to see you standing there when he opened his eyes."

He didn't respond.

The elevator doors opened, and we hurried down a long corridor, and I didn't have to wonder, "Which room?" There were two young cops from the Nineteenth Precinct standing outside the captain's door.

I rushed inside.

His chest was heavily bandaged, and his face was scraped and bruised from when he'd fallen on Forty-Fourth Street.

"You look like hell!" I said.

I leaned over and held him close.

"I don't care if this hurts."

"Neither do I," he agreed, which implied that it *did* hurt, so I let him go. Then I stood up straight, amazed that he seemed so alert.

"So," he kidded, "you couldn't walk six blocks to visit your uncle?"

Carlos, of course, had checked out every hospital in the metro area, over and over again, but somehow, when the captain was admitted, he'd been mistakenly assigned the name of a recently discharged patient, so the hospital staff had no record of either "Patrick Flanagan" or an unidentified "John Doe."

Instead, he was "Joseph Kurtz."

I kidded him right back.

"So Mr. Kurtz couldn't pick up the phone and call?"

He smiled and looked over at Carlos.

"Where's Sean Michael?"

"He's on his way. Some of the boys from the gym are driving him over."

The captain was relieved, but now it was time for *me* to get serious.

"Maybe it's time that the lying Flanagan brothers started telling the truth."

It was clear that my uncle was ready to talk.

"Have a seat, Sweetheart."

I did as I was told.

He explained.

Not long after Carmelita had sold her baby (me) to the champ, nineteen years ago, my old man, despite everything, was still hopeful that Carmelita would change her ways and come back to him. When he asked his brother to find her, my uncle agreed. Within a few weeks, he discovered that Carmelita Rivera had grown up in Santa Marta, Columbia, spending most of her youth on Caribbean beaches in the Tayrona National Park on Columbia's north shore. Those legendary beaches, generally considered among the most beautiful in South

America, are mostly isolated with only a few luxury hotels located in the vicinity.

Since the currents off Tayrona are particularly dangerous, the beaches in Tayrona are seldom used for swimming, so Carmelita grew up sunbathing, jet-skiing, and water-skiing. It was perfectly obvious to my uncle that Carmelita would never let herself get too far away from the ocean, so he started snooping around, calling in favors, and bribing contacts. Eventually, he managed to track her down in Acapulco.

Immediately, he flew to Mexico and confronted her on the beach. She was living in the condo of a wealthy actor, a Mexican soap star, and she was hitting the local beaches every day. She wasn't in the least bit intimidated by the captain's sudden appearance, and she actually seemed to enjoy the confrontation. She was totally dismissive of my uncle, and she maliciously ridiculed the champ.

"Fine," Uncle Pat warned her, "just stay out of his life."

She laughed. She clearly didn't like anyone telling her what to do, but on the other hand, she didn't have a problem with what he wanted.

"Why would I have anything to do with *his* life?" she asked sarcastically.

Then the captain paused, looking directly at me and Carlos from his hospital bed.

"You have to understand that the woman's a sociopath. She's essentially soulless. She's probably got an extreme type of Klüver-Bucy syndrome."

"What's that?" I asked.

"A *complete* lack of fear. I've only seen it twice in my life, and I sensed it immediately that day in Acapulco. Unlike the rest of us, she doesn't have a normal response to fear. No rapid heartbeat, no adrenaline, no increased respiration, none of the other things that the rest of us have to deal with in dangerous situations. The only reason I know about K-B is that I'd encountered it once with a serial rapist named Wilkins, and one of the specialists right here at Presbyterian tried to explain it to me. It's apparently related to some kind of damage or lesions in the medial lobes of the brain. Whatever that means."

"But isn't that just an excuse?" I said.

"Not from me! The woman's flat-out evil, and a lack of fear has nothing to do with that, but it definitely makes it easier for her to do the kinds of things she does."

I nodded, and my uncle continued.

After meeting with Carmelita on the beach in Acapulco, he flew back home and told my father that Carmelita was dead. He didn't like lying, but he wanted to put an end to everything, and it worked. The champ believed him, accepted her "death," and eventually moved on.

Two years later, the captain learned that Carmelita had murdered her mother at some resort in the Catskills and that she was about to stand trial at the Albany Courthouse. The same day, he drove to Albany and met with the Federal Prosecutor, Alan Carlyle, offering to testify if Carlyle would promise to keep his brother out of it. Since the case was already open-and-shut, Carlyle agreed.

"Why didn't my old man hear about the case?" I wondered. "After all, it was a matricide! The press must have been all over it."

"Yeah, it was *quite* a sensation in Albany," he agreed, "but the Markham murders were going on in Brooklyn at the same time. Besides, your father never watches the news anyway. All I had to do was keep an eye on the newspapers, which I did. Carefully. So he never knew."

"Then she ended up in Bedford Hills," I said.

He was impressed.

"I see that the two of you have been doing your homework!"

He finished the rest of the story.

Once Carmelita was safely locked away at Bedford Hills, my uncle asked an old friend who worked in the state penal system to keep an eye on her, and to update him whenever her parole hearings got started. Then last year, his old friend died of a heart attack, and his family had failed to notify the captain. In the meantime, Carmelita had cleverly arranged for her release from Bedford Hills.

A few days after Irina had fallen to her death in Times Square, the captain came back from Pittsburgh and saw the sketch of "Margarita" on his desk. Naturally, he knew who the woman was, and after a few quick phone calls, he arranged to meet with another old friend, an ex-cop who'd worked for a few years at Bedford Hills.

"Whom you met at Jimmy's Corner the night you were shot."

He smiled.

"Exactly."

"Did he tell you about the child?"

"Yes."

"Did you realize it was the girl in Times Square?"

"I wondered."

"Do you know who the father was?"

"No, but I'm sure we can find out."

"*Carlos* can find out. You're not going anywhere!"

Then the champ rolled into the room, looked at his brother, and all his worries instantly dissipated as he smiled his famous smile.

"Well," I said, "here comes the other liar."

26. Bedford Hills

I T WAS a pleasant drive.

Winding through lovely country roads.

Into Westchester County toward Bedford Hills.

As we entered the grounds, I wasn't afraid to admit that the place started giving me the creeps. In the past, I'd never had anything to do with "females," meaning female criminals, and I'd always done my best to avoid women's prisons, especially something like Bedford Hills, which was the largest women's prison in the state and the only one with maximum security.

Inside, as Dempsey and I made our way down prison corridors, I'd occasionally catch glimpses of some of the inmates out in the yard, or working or loafing in various rooms off the hallways. It's bad enough that so many men are violent, but this place was crammed with violent women, and it felt especially ugly. It felt wrong. What was the matter with these women? What were they doing with their lives? This was the place where they caged the famous female monsters:

Carolyn Warmus
Marybeth Tinning
Kathy Boudin
Sante Kimes
Pamela Smart

Most of whom were still here.

Finally, we arrived at the Warden's neat and isolated office. Dempsey, of course, had already checked him out, and so had Carlos. They both agreed that Lloyd Brockden seemed like a decent guy, who'd been doing the best he could in a thankless position for over twenty years. He was tall, graying, wearing a nondescript brown suit, and he was ready to cooperate. He even seemed remorseful about everything that had happened.

So what *had* happened?

Last August, after a riot in the south cellblock, one of the guards, John Alvarez, was taken hostage. Later, when the rebellion was shut down and everything was under control, Alvarez's body was found in a pool of blood.

His throat was slit.

"He was a good kid," the Warden explained, "with a wife and two small kids, and we wanted to do the right thing and give the family some closure."

But they had no leads.

None of the women would talk. Not one. Until Carmelita Rivera stepped forward. She said that she'd seen *everything* and that she'd name the murderer and testify in court for a reduced sentence.

"Naturally, we didn't want to make a deal with the likes of Rivera," Brockden explained, "but we felt we owed it to the Alvarez family. Besides, excepting her pregnancy many years earlier, she'd been a model inmate. She was clearly manipulative, but she was also a loner, and she'd kept herself out of trouble for over fifteen years. So we made the deal."

"Are you certain she gave you the right name?" Dempsey asked.

"Yes. I've still got my doubts about whether Rivera actually *saw* the murder, but the woman she named, Lucy Lexer, eventually confessed."

"Everything was by the book?" Dempsey asked.

"Yes. An open book. A slew of lawyers came down from Albany, and we cut the deal. Everything was on the up-and-up, but now I have to live with the consequences."

His regrets were obvious.

"I feel terrible about it."

I had no doubt that he was telling the truth, so I changed the subject.

"Tell us about the baby."

"That was about fifteen years ago," he remembered. "Rivera had only been here about two years."

"Who was the father?"

"A prison guard named Jason Parker."

As I expected.

"He was another good kid, but we had to fire him as soon as we found out the truth."

"I saw him murdered six days ago," I explained, "in Queens, at the Unisphere."

Which meant that both the father and his daughter had been killed on the same night.

Within a few hours of each other.

The same daughter who was also my sister.

The same daughter who was only fifteen years old.

The warden was stunned.

"Was it Rivera?"

"It seems that the killers worked for Carmelita."

I felt bad for the guy, but I needed more confirmation.

"What happened to the baby?"

"She ended up in the foster system," Brockden remembered. "I guess Carmelita kept tabs on her somehow."

"Under what name?"

"I don't know."

He thought things over.

"Are you *sure* she's the girl who fell in Times Square?"

"Yes," Dempsey assured him.

Now it was Dempsey's turn to change the subject.

"Do you have any idea where Carmelita might be?"

"No," he admitted. "I've been asking around, talking to some of the inmates who knew her, but all I can tell you is that she likes beaches, and she likes the ocean."

"There are a lot of beaches in the world," Dempsey pointed out.

The Warden nodded.

So did I.

27. Yankee Stadium

I WAS SITTING NEXT to Derek Jeter in the Yankees dugout.

I was lucky to have all kinds of modeling contracts, but the shoots for Major League Baseball were among my favorites. Sure, I loved showing off Armani or Versace gowns, but I was equally content wearing an "official/authentic" MLB jersey and smiling for the camera. I love baseball, but I was guilty of the most serious baseball *faux pas* that one can commit in New York City:

I rooted for *both* the Yankees and the Mets.

In New York, it's more acceptable to root for a non-city team (excepting, of course, the Red Sox) than to root for *both* the Mets and the Yankees at the same time. If you rooted for, say, the Cleveland Indians, then people would naturally assume that you'd had the terrible misfortune of living in Cleveland (or wherever) before you'd had the karma-esque good fortune to relocate to New York City. So rooting for the Indians would be seen as the consequence of something like a childhood misfortune or trauma, one that could be fully understood, if not fully condoned. But to root for both the Mets and the Yankees at the same time seemed to indicate some kind of innate inability to be a true fan, or to take a stand in life, or to choose between good and evil (depending, of course, on one's perspective).

Well, I didn't care. I grew up in a household that supported *all* the metro teams.

Mets/Yankees
Giants/Jets
Knicks/Nets
Rangers/Devils/Islanders

My dad was too much of a nice guy to root against any of the hometown teams, and I agreed. To hell with everyone else. I was perfectly content wearing a Yankees cap one day and a Mets cap the next.

Today I was wearing a Yankees cap.

Even though I was a "homer" (which was thoroughly discussed in my initial interview with MLB), I love baseball, *period*, and they were fine with that. I love what Babe Ruth once called the "beautiful" game, and I have absolutely no problem promoting any of the MLB teams and their jerseys (although I would have gladly foregone dressing in a dreaded Red Sox outfit).

So here I was, on a sunny afternoon in the Bronx in early July, posing for Dick Donaldson's Hasselblad in the empty but still magnificent ballpark. I love this place. The new stadium opened in 2009, but it was so closely modeled on the 1923 "House that Ruth Built" that the fans had nothing to complain about. Both the exterior and the interior looked very much the same, and even the distinctive frieze that lined the old roof had been replicated. As for the playing field dimensions, they were exactly the same:

Left field 318 (feet)
Left Center 399
Dead Center 408
Right Center 385
Right Field 314

Nevertheless, there was still a list of complaints: the $2.3 billion price tag, the taxpayer subsidies, the hyper-expensive "Legends Suite," as well as unfounded concerns that it might be some kind of "launching pad," like Coors Field in Denver or Turner Field in Atlanta. In life, there are always people complaining about everything, but I never paid any attention. I was perfectly happy that the park was marvelously beautiful.

The first Yankee to get a hit in the new stadium was, of course, Derek Jeter, in the Yankees's first exhibition game, a 7–4 win over the Cubs. Which was perfectly appropriate given that Jeter was the all-time Yankees hits leader, not to mention the all-time hits leader among shortstops. I've always liked Derek, whom I'd first met back in the days when he was dating a few of the well-known models in town, including Adriana Lima, before he dated Minka Kelly, who starred in the popular TV show *Friday Night Lights*.

So it was great fun sitting with an all-time great in the Yankees's dugout, smiling for the camera and promoting MLB caps and jerseys. It was a typical Dick Donaldson shoot: professional, comfortable, efficient, and relaxed. Dick didn't believe in panic. He believed in taking his time and getting things right. The only thing unusual about today's shoot was the presence of two NYPD cops standing near the infield, chatting with some of the security guys, keeping an eye out for potential assassins in the empty stadium.

Especially since Carlos wasn't there. Which felt peculiar since Carlos had become my shadow every minute of the day. He was even sleeping on a cot in the gym at the bottom of the stairs that lead to my apartment. He was *always* watching. *Always* protecting. But one of his closest cousins in Newark had just had a new baby girl, and I insisted that he go to New Jersey and visit the family. He'd gone reluctantly, of course, but I assured him that I'd have plenty of protection at Yankee Stadium.

Which I did.

It was now two weeks since Dempsey and I had gone to Bedford Hills and filled in the rest of the pieces in the Carmelita Rivera puzzle. But a number of questions still remained:

> *How did she convince Irina to kill Mitchell Carlyle?*
> *Did Carmelita push Irina off the roof?*
> *Did one of the Salazars do it?*
> *When was she coming after the captain again?*
> *When was she coming after the champ?*
> *When was she coming for me?*

The big question two weeks ago—Where *is* she?—was no longer a question. On the same day as Bedford Hills, Carlos had tracked the bulk of Ethan Walker's money to the Caymans, and the very next day, with me helping as much as I could, he ran cash tracers across every island in the Caribbean.

"Remember," I reminded him, "she liked Barbados."

But we found her on Martinique. She was living in a five-million-dollar beach house with two servants, a bodyguard (maybe Luis Salazar), a cook, and a maid. It was a smart choice. Martinique, officially, is an "overseas region" of France, and the French never extradite criminals to the US if the death penalty is a possible outcome, as in the famous case of the American murderer Ira Einhorn.

Given the fact that Carmelita had clearly arranged for the assassination of a US senator, the State Department had been putting a lot of pressure on the French, but they still weren't budging, insisting, as always, that they were taking the moral high ground on capital punishment. Dempsey, through his DC contacts, had learned that the State Department had offered to cut a deal that would have eliminated the death penalty, but the French still refused to cooperate.

Carmelita had won.

She was incredibly wealthy, living in a tropical paradise that was nine hundred miles across the Caribbean from the Tayrona beaches where she'd grown up in Columbia. Except for leaving the island, she could do whatever she wanted to do, and it seemed that she was spending most of her time sunbathing, jet-skiing, water-skiing, patronizing the best restaurants, and attending many of the island's upscale parties.

When the MLB photo shoot was finished, Derek and I, along with the cops and the security guys, went into the Yankees's locker rooms. Derek sat around for a bit, signing photographs and baseballs for the cops, and I got him talking about his famous walk-off homer in game four of the "November" series. He was modest as always, but eventually he had to get going. He stood up, took off my Yankees cap, playfully kissed the top of my head, and said goodbye.

When Derek was gone, I looked at the other guys, the four guys in uniform.

"It's time to change, boys," I said.

The men nodded, smiled, or both, then they left me alone in the spacious locker room. I'd already decided to wear my Yankees jersey home, but I wanted to swap my baseball pants for the pretty Lauren skirt that I'd worn to the stadium. After I made the switch, I started to collect my things.

Then I heard it.

A soft thump.

It was exactly what I'd been expecting for the past two weeks, and I knew exactly what it meant. I also knew where my weapon was. For the past two weeks, my Glock was *always* within arm's reach. Even when Dick Donaldson was clicking away in the Yankees dugout, my open tote was right beside me on the bench.

I heard another thump.

A suppressor sound.

I grabbed my Glock and wondered where I should position myself in the locker room.

It was too late.

A man wearing a Yankee Stadium Security uniform came around the corner of the doorway. He was carrying a SIG P220 with a muzzle suppressor, most probably a Nexus eight-inch silencer.

It seemed that Luis Salazar wasn't in Martinique after all. He was right *here* in the bowels of Yankee Stadium looking for me.

He lifted his weapon, and I shot him through the right shoulder. His shoulder jerked a bit, but he still held onto his weapon, seemingly unconcerned. Salazar, I had no doubt, was the man who'd shot my uncle in the back, and the brother of the man I'd killed at Storm King Cabins.

He had exactly the same look in his eyes as his brother.

Which said:

"You'll have to kill me. There's no other way."

I would have preferred a headshot, although momentarily, I did consider a 9 mm straight through the heart, but instead, I shot him twice more, once in each thigh, as he collapsed to the ground, still holding his SIG P220.

"Let it go," I heard myself say, with astonishing calmness.

But Salazar wouldn't let go of his weapon, so I shot him through the wrist, and the gun fell from his hand. Cautiously, I walked over, with my Glock pointed directly at his slumped head, and I kicked the gun away. Outside, in the corridor, I could hear people rushing toward me, and I suddenly felt safe again. Then I remembered what Luis Salazar had done to my uncle, and before I realized what I was doing, I kicked him in the face.

28. "The Case of the Terrified Typist"

I N THE CALIFORNIA DARKNESS, a car drives to the edge of a pier, and a man gets out and quickly dumps a body into the Pacific Ocean. Nearby, an old wharf rat is sitting in a dinghy, witnessing everything.

Or did he?

"Pause it right there," the captain called out.

The champ, always at the controls, did as his brother requested. Then the two of them argued vigorously and fruitlessly about whether the old guy could have actually seen the face of the man who'd dumped the body in the darkness. In truth, it was completely "immaterial," as Hamilton Berger might have put it, as were almost all of their good-natured arguments.

Normally, we did our *Perry Mason* screenings in order, in the exact sequence that they'd originally appeared on CBS from

1957 to 1966, but last night another pointless argument had somehow segued into this particular argument, and the only way they could resolve the issue was to rewatch "The Case of the Terrified Typist," which was actually from season one, thus out of its normal sequence.

I sat on the couch eating M&Ms, enjoying the brothers' nonsensical debate about the least interesting aspect of "The Terrified Typist," which was one of Perry Mason's most fascinating and complex cases. One of only three cases that Perry actually lost! As it turned out, he ended up defending Duane Jefferson, the same guy who'd tossed the body off the pier into the Pacific Ocean. After Jefferson's conviction in the courtroom, Perry figured out that the guy was an imposter. Then he located and released the real Duane Jefferson, who'd been kidnapped, and by the end of the show, despite his loss in the courtroom, Perry had completely solved the complicated case. It was also clear that Perry's bogus client, with another lawyer defending him, would eventually be convicted again, having now been charged with blackmail, kidnapping, conspiracy, and perjury.

As well as murder!

"Well, what do *you* think, Deirdre?" one of the Flanagans asked.

It was apparently time for the great decider to pass judgment.

"I think you're both idiots! There are many other *far more* interesting and questionable aspects of this case. For example, has the audience been given enough information to follow Perry's deductions about the kidnapping? But since I'm obligated to render a summary judgment, I'll give this one to the champ."

"What?" said the captain, slapping his bottle of Guinness down on the tabletop, just as he always did whenever my decisions went against him, which neither of the dopey brothers ever noticed was *exactly* fifty percent of the time.

"I think," I continued, ignoring my uncle, "that the champ's arguments were remarkably weak, especially all that excessive praise regarding the 'camera angle' on the wharf rat's dinghy, but his overall perception still seems accurate: the identification *could* have been made from thirty-five feet."

My verdict, of course, gave them both something to be pleased about. The champ would be satisfied that he was correct, and the captain would be similarly satisfied that he'd presented the better arguments.

One of them had once been the super-middleweight champion of the world, and the other one was now a much-decorated captain at NYPD, yet they both acted like children whenever they were together. Yesterday afternoon, I'd nearly been killed at Yankee Stadium, and today they were, once again, arguing about a *Perry Mason* episode, and I was truly grateful for their remarkable resilience, for their determination to try and keep our lives as normal as possible. Or whatever might pass for "normal" at Flanagan's Gym.

Moments like these, I knew, were the best moments of my life, and I appreciated every single minute. I'd like to believe that I've always been what others called a "grateful" kind of person, but after the past few weeks, it was especially easy to realize just how wonderful my life truly was, and just how wonderful these two old men were. Even when they were lying to protect someone they loved.

Oddly enough, over the past two weeks, even though we'd been extremely vigilant, the brothers hadn't said much about Carmelita, but now that Luis Salazar was in custody, they did their best to be hopeful that Carmelita would finally forget about New York City, forget about revenge and the Flanagans, and live out her life in paradise.

As for Salazar, he was still nursing his wounds at St. Barnabas in the Bronx. Since his SIG P220 clearly matched the slug taken from the captain's back, he'd eventually admitted to the shooting outside Jimmy's Corner. Naturally, he denied having anything to do with any of the other killings, putting all the blame on his dead brother, while making it perfectly clear that Carmelita ran the show. He explained that, in the beginning, he and his brother had been lured into her schemes by money. She had "lots and lots of money." But later, he claimed, they were actually afraid of her.

"Yeah, right," Dempsey scoffed.

"You don't know the woman," Salazar insisted. "She's not like other people. There's something missing. She's colder than cold, and she really spooked us when she told us what she'd done."

"What was that?"

"Slit her mother's throat with a knife."

Later Dempsey told me that he believed the guy. Luis Salazar and his brother Antonio were stone-cold killers, but they were still afraid of Carmelita Rivera.

My mother.

Luis had admitted to shooting a New York City cop in the back, and even if they didn't get him on anything else, he'd be packed off to Sing Sing until the day he died, while Carmelita was enjoying life on a sunny beach in Martinique, drinking piña coladas.

Technically, the Carmelita Rivera case was still open, but despite the efforts of the State Department, everyone knew it was really closed.

I popped an M&M greenie in my mouth and watched as Perry and Berger went at it in the courtroom:

> Mr. Berger: *Your Honor, this is just another wild-eyed dramatic grandstand play for which counsel is so noted.*

But I was really thinking about Carmelita. My mother. She was now two thousand miles away, but she'd already achieved much of her revenge:

> *Alan Carlyle, the prosecutor in her murder case*
> *Mitchell Carlyle, the prosecutor's son*
> *Keith Palmero, her defense attorney*
> *Jason Parker, the man who'd fathered her second child*
> *Irina Parker, her own daughter*

Now, it seemed, there were only "three" left, all with the same last name, and I knew that it would *never* be over, and so did everyone else, and there was only one person who could do anything about it.

Me.

29. Martinique

I SAT IN THE BACK of the cabin cruiser staring through a pair of Zeiss binoculars. The cruiser was making a pass off the coast of Les Salines, and I was scanning the white sandy beaches near Sainte-Anne.

I was looking for my mother.

"There she is," I said to Carlos, who was sitting nearby.

Carmelita was lying topless on the beach behind her plantation-styled mansion. She looked like she was twenty-five years old, lying on a yellow towel, wearing a white straw hat, roasting herself in the Caribbean sunshine near a stand of coconut trees. From this far away, it seemed to be a scene of perfect idyllic contentment.

I'd seen enough.

I offered the binoculars to Carlos, but he shook his head. He had no interest. He was completely focused on tonight, and he didn't approve of our little excursion around the island, but I wanted to get a peek at Carmelita's domain. Maybe even catch a glimpse of the monster herself.

Carlos wasn't worried that we'd be spotted. After all, we were too far away, just one of many pleasure crafts gliding past Les Salines in the hot afternoon. Besides, we'd probably passed by Carmelita's mansion in less than a minute or two.

As always, Carlos had given in.

He certainly understood my natural curiosity, maybe even my natural compulsion, so he agreed to make the arrangements for our little excursion. His only concern was that I might believe that getting a look at Carmelita might, in some way, explain something.

Elucidate something.

It didn't, of course, and I knew it wouldn't.

We cruised around the rest of the island in silence, staring, like spellbound tourists, at its lush and breathtaking beauty. Christopher Columbus, its European discoverer, once described the island as one of the most beautiful places he'd ever seen. Even today, it seemed almost completely covered with thick green vegetation, bright colorful wildflowers, and endless fruits. Mangoes, papayas, lemons, limes, pineapples, bananas, and West Indian cherries. Like Les Salines, all the spectacular southern beaches were perfectly complemented by the magnificent mountains in the north, especially Mount Pelée.

Yet even in Paradise, even on Martinique, darkness lies in wait. On May 8, 1902, with no warning, Mount Pelée suddenly erupted, split itself in two, and began spewing out poisonous gases and burning black ash. Within seconds, molten lava was racing toward the capital city, Saint-Pierre, known in those days as "The Paris of the West Indies." Scientists have claimed that the lava reached speeds of 250 miles per hour, with a temperature of 3,600 degrees. Within two minutes, all 30,000 inhabitants of Saint-Pierre were dead.

Vaporized.

Even here, within this tropical paradise, there was danger and death and evil. Now it was lying on the glittering white-sand beach at Les Salines.

Two days earlier, I'd lied to my father, telling him that I was leaving the next day for a three-day shoot in Montreal for Calvin Klein

Sabrina agreed to cover for me.

"What's up?" she wondered.

It was natural curiosity, not an accusation.

"The old man'll worry too much if he thinks I'm taking a break at Mount Hood," I lied, referring to my cover story. "Only an ex-boxer would worry about some harmless snowboarding in Oregon with my girlfriends."

We both laughed, and my old man, eventually, agreed to the "Montreal shoot."

"Take Carlos along," he insisted.

"I've already asked him."

"Good."

Last night, Carlos and I flew to Le Lamentin International Airport, just east of Martinique's present-day capital, Fort-de-France. Under normal circumstances, I would have preferred to be just a regular tourist, exploring every aspect of this lovely island. I would have visited St. Louis Cathedral, toured one of the sugarcane plantations, then browsed through the Paris fashions in the countless boutiques on Rue Victor Schoelcher. But not on this trip. We needed to keep a low profile, and the only time we actually left our rooms at Hôtel La Batelière was for the short boat cruise around the island.

Approaching the pretty coastal town of Bellefontaine, I glanced over at Carlos. He was wearing, as was typical, one of his dark-blue button-down dress shirts, with white buttons, with dark shades, with polarized lenses. He looked like a celebrity, like some kind of Latin rock star, and I knew that every girl on the island of Martinique (every girl on the island of Manhattan for that matter) would have loved for the likes of Carlos Menendez to stroll into her life. But Carlos, as you know, insisted on being in love with me, which was totally unfair, totally useless, totally pointless. I wished that I could do something about it, but I didn't know what.

Like Dempsey, who was flying to the island later tonight, Carlos seemed oddly content with the status quo, the way things were. Both of them were stoics. I can't remember either one of them complaining about anything, and I wished that I could say the same about myself. They were both good men. Exceptional. Except for my old man and my uncle, they were the two best men I'd ever met.

In no uncertain terms, I'd told them both that it was ridiculous, an absolute dead end, but they both just shrugged and didn't say a word. I suppose they both hoped that things would eventually change, but they wouldn't. I was certain about that. As a matter of fact, I'd never even allowed myself to speculate about either might-have-beens or might-still-happens. What *was* at present, though perfectly unsatisfactory, was the way it was going to be.

The cruiser pulled into the bay and docked at one of the marinas at Fort-de-France. It was now time to get back to the hotel and prepare for tonight's reception.

Four hours later, at seven o'clock sharp, I arrived at the Dutch Consulate at 44 Avenue Maurice Bishop. I was dressed in a sleek, black Versace gown with a draped bodice, and I was accompanied by Marc Vallée, the capital city's retired chief of police. Vallée, a man in his mid-sixties, still wore his tux quite well, and he seemed delighted to be serving as tonight's escort for a young American model, even though we were both fully aware that there'd be no time for socializing at the party this evening.

Tonight's reception was being held in honor of Gerolt Van der Meer, the well-known Dutch novelist who was visiting from the Netherlands. Since Van der Meer often set his novels in the Windward Islands, he was very popular in the West Indies, and tonight's guest list included a who's who of elite Martinique society: politicians, artists, diplomats, wealthy Béké aristocrats, and of course, Madame Carmelita Rivera.

The plan, which I'd concocted two weeks ago, was rather simple.

The Dutch Consulate and its grounds were, technically, *not* considered French soil, and the Dutch had a workable extradition treaty with the United States. So I convinced Dempsey, through his contacts at the State Department, to see if the Dutch would be willing to take Carmelita into custody if she were properly arrested. Through various back channels, they eventually agreed, with the proviso that they'd have no public involvement with the arrest.

The State Department told Dempsey essentially the same thing:

His contact: *We can't go bursting into consulates and grabbing people, Rick.*

Dempsey: *I understand.*

[Pause]

His contact: *Contact Mark Vallée. He'll be able to get her off the island.*

Dempsey: *Anything else?*

His contact: *Yeah, just remember that we're not part of any of this.*

Dempsey (kidding): *Part of what?*

His contact (kidding): *It's been nice not talking to you.*

So Dempsey got in touch with Monsieur Vallée, who was glad to help. As it turned out, he greatly admired Senator Carlyle, whom he'd met several years ago in New York City, and he was also a close friend of the Dutch ambassador, and they made arrangements for a "silent" extradition.

Unless Carmelita created a scene at the reception, everything was to be handled discreetly. At some point in the evening, she'd be invited to the consulate's library, where Vallée, acting as an official agent of the United States, more specifically the City of New York, would place her under arrest. She'd then be detained for the night, in a comfortable but secure suite within the consulate, and early tomorrow morning, she'd be quickly, efficiently, hustled out of the country before anything hit the web or the newspapers. Vallée had arranged for a private jet, departing at seven fifteen in the morning, with me and Carlos on board.

My job, which I'd assigned myself, was rather dull. I was to sit, unseen, at a front window in the consulate and positively identify Carmelita when she arrived at the reception.

I love parties, and I'd dressed appropriately for the occasion, as had Vallée, so we could blend in if necessary, but tonight, I was more than willing to forego the socializing.

When we arrived at the consulate, everything was ready, and Vallée and I took our positions.

Waiting.

Forever.

But Carmelita never showed up.

For three hours, we sat in attentive silence, hoping with every arriving car or limousine that Carmelita was about to make an appearance.

"Maybe she's running late," Vallée would occasionally say, with his charming French accent, but by ten o'clock, neither of us believed it anymore.

What went wrong?

Maybe it was just a coincidence.

Maybe Carmelita had decided, for whatever reason, not to bother with another party tonight. Or maybe she was cautious. Careful. Maybe she'd made up her mind to *never ever* step off French soil again, not even into a foreign consulate.

Or maybe she'd anticipated everything.

I wouldn't put it past her.

"Maybe we should join the party?" Vallée suggested. "You deserve it."

I appreciated his kindness, but I wasn't ready to give up.

Not yet.

"You go ahead," I insisted. "I'll stay here for another half hour or so, watching at my window, sipping champagne."

Vallée stood up, bowed politely, and left the unlit room. I hung around until ten forty-five, when I finally faced the fact that my clever little scheme had imploded.

Maybe it was time to contact Carlos, who was stationed outside, and tell him to come inside so we could join the party.

Why not?

Since I'd foolishly splashed a few drops of champagne on my wrist, I decided to find a ladies' room to wash off the stickiness before I called Carlos.

I left the library and found a ladies' room, which was large and empty. I washed my hands and looked at my face in the mirror. If I was going to a party, I wanted to look my best.

Then a figure appeared behind me in the mirror. He was tall, powerful, wearing a gray suit. Instantly, in complete silence, I was overpowered. Despite my attempt to resist, he taped my mouth and bound my hands with copper wire. I tried reaching into my evening bag, of course, but everything had happened too quickly.

It was efficient.

Violent.

He lifted me off the ground, over his shoulder, and carried me out the back door of the bathroom, down an empty corridor, exiting the back entrance of the consulate. I made desperate attempts to resist, but it was useless. Then I realized that he had an accomplice, another silent man in a gray suit, who was walking behind us, carrying my Gucci handbag.

Frightened, helpless, I decided that it was best to conserve my strength.

With no hesitation, with amazing speed, I was carried across the back lawn of the consulate, down a shrub-lined path, through a small gate, into a large, enclosed garden with a view of the Caribbean. I had no doubt that we were now on French soil. The man suddenly stopped and set me down on my feet. In front of Carmelita. Who stood, rather majestically, in front of the distant moonlit ocean, not far from a black Mercedes Benz.

She looked lovely.

Stunning.

She wore a short designer dress, maybe Ralph Lauren, with a tropical floral print, mostly green, with some yellows, oranges, and blues.

She was smiling.

She nodded at my abductor, who ripped the tape from my mouth.

She didn't say, "Nobody'll hear you if you scream," since it was obvious. Instead, she looked me up and down as if I were something odd and curious, yet not quite acceptable.

Once again, I sensed the detachment, the distance, the same unsettling disassociation that I'd sensed four weeks ago on the terrace of the Donna Karan showroom.

What Uncle Pat called "soullessness."

What Luis Salazar called "colder than cold."

She smiled.

"You're most persistent," she said, with her intoxicating Columbian accent, "just like your mother."

Meaning herself.

There were, of course, a million things I would have liked to ask the deranged woman who was, apparently, my own mother.

All I could manage was:

"What's wrong with you?"

It was clearly accusatory, but it was also sincere. I wanted to know, and I wondered if she knew the answer herself.

She shrugged.

"I won't be wronged," she said, as if that explained everything. "I've been wronged in my life."

"That's just an excuse! *Everybody's* been 'wronged' in their life. What about my father? What did he ever do to you?"

"Nothing," she agreed, "and that's exactly the problem. When I was up there rotting in that hellhole in Westchester County, he never came to visit me. Not once."

"He didn't even know you were there."

"Well, he *should* have. He *should* have. It's what's known as the sin of omission, *mi querida*, and he'll pay for it. His brother too."

I was getting nowhere. The woman was obviously out of her mind.

I glanced at my silent captors, both in their mid-forties, probably French-speaking thugs from the island. I wondered if they were brothers, like the Salazars, and I wondered if they were also afraid of the woman who stood before us.

As was I.

"If you're looking for Signor Menendez," she explained, "he's in the trunk of the car. Maurice had to taser him six times. He's quite the tough guy."

Fear, in a wave of nausea, overwhelmed me.

A wave of weakness.

"Is he alive?"

I was panicked.

She smiled. She seemed to be enjoying herself.

"For the moment."

Carmelita looked at the beautiful dark ocean as if to indicate where Carlos would end up.

Where *I* would also end up.

"Now it's your turn, little lady," she said matter-of-factly, "but don't worry, it'll be quite painless."

Not yet.

"Who pushed my sister off the roof?" I called out.

She stared into my eyes.

"*I* did, of course."

Then she nodded to her thugs, and the one who'd carried me from the ladies' room stepped behind me, put his hands around my neck, and drove me down to my knees. His power, his ever-tightening grip, was completely overwhelming. I was helpless.

Then the second man stepped forward with my handbag and handed it to Carmelita. She looked inside, smiled at the Glock, then turned back to the second man.

"*Rapidement*," she said.

Without emotion.

The second man stepped beside me, pointing his weapon at my face. It looked like a Taurus Millennium. Everything was happening too fast. It seemed like a dream and my mind went blank. I attempted to struggle from the other man's grasp, but it was useless.

I thought of my father.

It felt as though I were abandoning him.

A voice called out of the darkness.

"Don't move!"

The voice came from behind us.

Then repeated itself in French, "*Ne faites pas un geste!*"

Dempsey stepped forward into the moonlight with his weapon focused on the man with the Taurus.

"Toss it."

The man did as he was told.

"Let her go," Dempsey called to the other man.

The man standing behind me immediately released his grip, and I slumped forward gagging a bit.

In the meantime, Dempsey quickly cuffed the men together and forced them to lie facedown on the shaded grass in front of Carmelita.

"My Glock's in the purse!" I called out, rising from my knees.

"Drop it," Dempsey called out to Carmelita.

She hesitated.

"If you think I won't shoot," he warned her, "you have no idea who I am."

"I know who you are," she assured him, with a curious mixture of placidity and venom.

It seemed as though she'd just added Dempsey to her "murder list."

She dropped the handbag, standing alone in the moonlight. She was lovely, still supremely confident, even though her tight summer dress made it perfectly clear that she wasn't carrying a handgun.

Suddenly, everyone was startled by several loud thumps from the trunk of the Mercedes. Everyone except Carmelita. As Dempsey was momentarily distracted, one of the men lying on the ground kicked him in the leg, and Carmelita stepped forward. As if from nowhere, there was a knife in her hand, and I saw it rising into the moonlight over Dempsey.

Instinctively, I bent down.

I'd been waiting for the chance all night, wondering if I'd ever get the opportunity.

I slipped my hands, still bound, beneath the hem of my gown, and located my "Baby Glock."

The twenty-two-ounce subcompact was taped to the back of my right calf.

Just as my uncle had taught me.

"For dangerous situations, Sweetheart."

The knife began to descend toward Dempsey's neck.

I retrieved my weapon.

This was definitely one of those situations.

Where someone I loved was in danger.

I fired once and the 9 mm entered through Carmelita's right temple, blew through her brain, and exited out the left temple into the moonlit darkness.

A headshot.

No ifs, no ands, no buts.

Carmelita, still holding the knife, fell backward into the blackness of the garden, laying herself down, almost comfortably, so she could see the distant beach, the distant ocean.

Then with my hands still taped together in front of me, still holding my Baby Glock, I walked over and looked down at the dead body of my mother.

She was beautiful.

Except for the stream of blood gushing from her right temple.

30. Midtown South

I'D LIKE TO TALK to Deirdre," my uncle said. "Alone."

Dempsey stood up and left the captain's office.

It was two days after the death of Carmelita in Martinique, and this was the "post-mortem" in New York City. Dempsey and I had just finished explaining everything, in detail, to my uncle, who'd listened in total silence.

We explained the plan, what happened, and the aftermath.

How Dempsey, with his cell, had contacted Marc Vallée, who was still at the reception. How Vallée rushed to the scene of the shooting, taking charge. How he hustled Carmelita's two thugs into custody, working a deal with the Martinique police force, smoothing things over at the consulate. How he even managed to keep the three Americans out of it.

The next day, *France-Antilles*, Martinique's only daily, had a brief item about the "robbery-gone-wrong" death of Madame Carmelita Rivera, who'd recently moved to the island and was living at Cul-de-Sac du Marin in Les Salines. The next day (early this morning), the State Department released a brief statement verifying that the woman killed in Martinique in the "robbery-gone-wrong" was the same woman being sought in connection with the assassination of Senator Alan Carlyle. The motive for the senator's murder was, apparently, revenge for a homicide conviction in the Albany courthouse seventeen years ago. Since the actual assassin in the death of Senator Carlyle, Antonio Salazar, had already been killed in a related incident at Storm King, New York, the case was now closed.

My name was never mentioned.

"You OK?" the captain asked.

Which was his first concern.

"Yes."

"You sure? We've got counselors in the building. With absolute confidentiality."

I was glad he didn't say, "Look, Sweetheart, you're just a nineteen-year-old girl, you were nearly murdered two nights ago, and you still have strangle marks and bruises on your neck. Maybe you need to talk to someone."

Or, "Look, Sweetheart, you're a nineteen-year-old girl, and you've shot and killed two people in the last two weeks, and one of them was your own mother. Are you sure you don't need to talk to someone?"

"If I need to talk to someone," I assured him, "I'll talk with you."

Which was, I felt certain, the perfect answer, and the captain just nodded.

The truth was, I didn't know how I felt. It was much too soon. All I knew was that I'd been fortunate to do what I'd set out to do:

help Midtown discover who'd pushed the young girl in the red dress off the roof at Times Square. The fact that the young girl was my half sister, and that the murderer was not, as one might have anticipated, some perversely sexed vicious male, but was instead my own mother, was at this point, beyond my comprehension.

Things had happened too fast for me to fathom what kind of damage it might have done to my psyche, my inner self, my soul. For now, I was just relieved that it was over, and that the ones I loved—my old man, my uncle, Carlos, and Dempsey—were safe.

In New York City.

"It was foolish, Deirdre," the captain continued, and I agreed with him.

Not because the plan was fundamentally flawed, but because Carmelita was too smart. Too clever. Ever since I was kidnapped two nights ago, I'd been wondering whether *everything* had been a setup.

Maybe Carmelita had chosen French Martinique with the specific intention of luring me to the island. Maybe she realized, as soon as she opened the engraved invitation from the Dutch Consulate, that something was up. Maybe she even knew that Carlos and I were staying at Hôtel La Batelière, and that we'd hired a local sea-pilot with a thirty-eight-foot cabin cruiser to buzz around the island to get a closer look.

Who could possibly know what Carmelita knew?

"She was too smart," I admitted to my uncle.

The captain nodded again, looking at me intently.

"I want you to promise that you'll never do anything like this again. At least, not without telling me first."

He said it without any real sense of authority. He spoke desperately, as if begging, and I felt sorry for him. I fully understood his concern, his emotions, but I decided to answer honestly.

"I promise," I agreed. "Unless your life's in danger. Or the champ's."

It wasn't the answer he wanted, but he knew it would have to do. He was still worried and fearful, and his love for me was palpable.

It filled the room.

"I love you, Uncle Pat."

"I know."

It was all he could say.

We sat there for a few moments, alone, in the silence of his office, grateful to be together, grateful to be alive, grateful to be heading back toward some kind of normalcy.

"I'm not telling the champ," I said.

There was no need for my old man to know that I'd had anything to do with the death of Carmelita Rivera.

It was over.

Finally.

It would have to be yet another secret in the Flanagan household, but it was a secret that I believed in.

So did my uncle.

"Good idea."

31. Cornell Medical Center

DIRECT FROM ST. PAT'S, as I did every Sunday, I walked through the front doors of the Cornell Medical Center on East Sixty-Eighth Street, took the elevator to the tenth floor, and walked down the main corridor of the Whitney Wing to Room 1032.

I was dressed in exactly the same clothes that I'd worn three years, two months, and six days ago:

> *A white, mostly cotton summer dress from Tommy*
> *Hilfiger, with a red cloth belt*
> *Light green Mary Janes, with matching green*
> *Hilfiger handbag*

I looked, I believed, as attractive as I could possibly look, even though he couldn't see me, even though he himself would look exactly the same as he'd looked last week: flat out on his hospital bed, covered to the chest with a clean white sheet, slightly raised at the head, attached to various monitors and IVs.

Comatose.

His name was Dr. Vincente Ramon Ramirez.

My husband.

We'd met three years, two months, and six days ago in the same hospital, down on the fourth floor of the Weill Center. I'd stopped by that day to visit my uncle, who was being checked out for a worrisome arrhythmia. When I found Uncle Pat, he was wearing a white hospital gown, standing on the fourth-floor veranda, talking to his cardiologist about his encouraging test results.

I walked up to the two men.

I was only sixteen at the time, never been kissed, and dressed in my Hilfigers. When the captain saw me, he smiled:

"Hey, Sweetheart. This is the doctor I've told you about."

It was true that my uncle had mentioned, in passing, something about a "very nice" doctor, but I'd mostly forgotten about it, even though it seemed rather odd at the time. Generally, the Flanagan brothers spent every single minute of every single waking hour scaring off anything that might possibly be a potential boyfriend.

Essentially saying:

"If you're looking at my daughter (or my niece), just remember that I was once super-middleweight champion of the world (or that I'm an NYPD captain who carries a Glock 34/35 twenty-four hours a day)."

They'd even, of course, concocted the whole HSDD syndrome myth, which was fine with me. I appreciated all their protections, and I wasn't really looking for boyfriends.

I was only sixteen.

I had plenty of time for that.

Vincente turned around, we looked at each other, and nothing was ever the same. I was much too young to actually believe in things like "flashes of lightning," "electricity," or "getting knocked off your feet." Even though I was a much pampered "girl's girl," I'd grown up in a world of men, and I'd never quite figured out how Elizabeth, in *Pride and Prejudice*, had managed to reverse herself about Darcy.

I didn't worry about it too much.

"Your uncle's told me a lot about you," the doctor said, speaking with what I'd later learn was an Argentine accent, "so I suppose I'm already in love with you."

I didn't know what to say, and the captain didn't like it one bit.

"Hey, I don't like the sound of that," he said in his cop voice, wondering what kind of Pandora's box he might have just opened.

The doctor and I shook hands, politely. Then Vincente turned back to the captain, trying, somehow, to mitigate his effusiveness.

"Forgive me, Sir," he said, sounding like something from a Jane Austen novel, "but maybe you've told me too much that seems exactly right."

I've always believed that the captain, instantly, made a mental note to never, under any circumstances, praise his niece to an unmarried male over the age of sixteen and under the age of thirty-five.

Make that fifty.

Nevertheless, it was already too late.

The doctor lifted the captain's test results and returned to fibrillations and tachycardias as I just stood there, knowing full well what the doctor was really thinking about, suspecting that he was also aware that I was thinking about nothing but him.

Forty-six minutes later, he called me on my cell phone, and the whirlwind began. Now, more than three years later, what happened back then seems like a perfect frenzy of perfect happiness. Over and over, Vincente, who was thirty-two years old at the time, offered to back off. After all, I was only sixteen, which might have been acceptable in Argentina, but as he fully understood, not here in Manhattan.

I didn't care, so I put an end to it.

"I don't want to hear that again," I told him firmly, and I never heard it again.

Of course, I'd heard about Latin lovers, and at first I wondered if there was such a thing as "Argentine lovers," but Vincente was always perfectly respectful, always putting me first, always submitting to my wishes.

Which meant, of course, not telling the champ.

In my heart, I truly believed, without a doubt, that my father would have gladly approved if I had been twenty-one years old. After all, Vincente had grown up in a serious family of physicians in Buenos Aires, all of whom were respected in their community, in their diocese, in Argentine medical circles. Just like his father, Vincente had gone to medical school at Cornell, learning the most up-to-date cardiological treatments and surgical methodologies, and until we met, he was planning to return to Argentina, meet a nice girl from Buenos Aires, and spend the rest of his life saving lives. It all seemed rather simple until I showed up in my Tommy Hilfigers.

Two months later, when I was supposedly on a *Marie Claire* shoot in the Florida Keys, we eloped to San Juan, got married at Convento de los Dominicos, then honeymooned at Condado Plaza Hotel. Arm in arm, we walked down the cobblestoned streets of old San Juan, beneath the balustraded balconies, beneath the lush hanging plants. We strolled the Paseo de la Princesa, visited El Morro and the Catedral de San Juan Bautista, dropped a few bucks at the Condado Casino, and enjoyed the beaches of Playa del Condado.

I'd never been more certain about anything in my life, and I knew that the champ would eventually accept everything when I turned eighteen. In two years. When I'd walk into his office someday, shut the door, and tell him the most important thing in my life. In the meantime, my wedding ring was safely hidden in the lowest drawer of my bureau, right next to my old copy of *The Life and Legacy of Annie Oakley*.

I'd explain to the champ that the elopement had been *my* decision. That we planned to live in the city, close to the gym.

The champ would understand.

I had no doubts.

Two weeks after we left San Juan, Vincente was "crashed and rolled" on the West Side Highway. The roof of his Infiniti was crushed, and they had to pry him out of the wreck. His head was severely concussed and traumatized, and he hasn't been conscious since. For the first six months, I was at his bedside every single day, still not telling the champ, accepting it as my own personal trial, my own personal cross.

I was all alone.

No one knew.

Not even Vincente's family knew the truth. The *whole* truth. They visited as often as they could, and they were convinced by Dr.

Kaplan that their son shouldn't be moved, that he was getting the best possible treatment at Cornell Medical Center. He also convinced them, at my request, that Vincente's stupendous medical bills were covered by his health insurance plan, which were *really* covered, barely, by my modeling assignments. So the grieving parents, who believed that I was Vincente's girlfriend at the time of the accident, agreed to leave him right where he was.

Much to my relief.

So *no one* knew.

Except, of course, Dr. Kaplan.

Now, in the fourth year, I stopped by as often as I could, and I *always* came on Sunday afternoons. It was a ritual of sorts.

A ritual of love.

I would walk into the room, kiss my husband, and tell him that I loved him and missed him.

Then I'd hold his hand until Dr. Kaplan arrived at exactly one fifteen to discuss exactly the same things we always discussed. When the doctor was finished, I'd go over to the window and look outside. Then I'd return to the bed, sit down, and read from Borges, just as we'd done on our honeymoon in San Juan. Sometimes I'd read Borges's wonderful sonnets, sometimes I'd read his exquisite short stories. Since my Spanish was perfunctory, I'd read from the best English translations. Today, I was planning to begin "*La muerte y la brújula,*" "Death and the Compass," as translated "masterfully," as Vincente had once put it, by Anthony Kerrigan.

Appropriately enough, it was the story of a vengeance-minded criminal who ingeniously lures the clever detective, Erik Lönnrot, into a trap at Trieste-le-Roy.

The story begins:

Of the many problems which exercised the daring
perspicacity of Lönnrot none was so strange—so harshly
strange, we may say—as the staggered series of bloody acts
which culminated at the villa of Trieste-le-Roy, amid the
boundless odor of the eucalypti.

At five-thirty, I would kiss my husband again, leave the hospital, and meet with the other two men in my life for our regular Sunday "eat-out," often at one of the Brazilian restaurants on Forty-Sixth Street. Tonight, I was meeting the boys at my personal favorite, Ipanema, between Fifth and Sixth, where I could sip a cool Caipirinha and order the specialty of the house.

Feijoada Completa.

"How are you, Deirdre?" Dr. Kaplan asked at one fifteen.

I liked and much admired the doctor. He was honest, efficient, and he never wasted time. Yet underneath his professional demeanor, the doctor was a truly compassionate caring man. He seemed, as if in some personal way, to understand what it was like to have a loved one in a nonresponsive condition, but I never intruded into his personal life, always respecting his privacy.

"I'm well," I responded, as I always did.

Then the doctor discussed the fact, as he always did, that nothing had changed since he'd seen me last Sunday. Nothing was better. Nothing was worse. Although, of course, no one could ever really know for sure.

Dr. Kaplan, who'd known and admired Vincente when they were colleagues at the Weill Center, was always gently preparing me for the worst, yet he was still willing to admit that Vincente might last exactly as he was for years, even admitting that, "Yes, there *are* cases" where similar patients in similar circumstances have inexplicably revived, even though it was one in a million, then lived out somewhat normal healthy lives.

Once a month, the doctor would make a point of telling me, gently, that it was important for me to get on with the rest of my life, even though it was never perfectly clear exactly what he meant.

We were both aware that his vagueness was intentional.

Fortunately, not today.

It wasn't one of those Sundays.

I thanked the doctor, sincerely, and he left the room.

Then I rose from my chair, stepped over to the window, and looked down into the hospital parking lot near the East River. It was easy, as always, to spot the coolest car in Manhattan, a '73 Trans Am Firebird with a Screaming Chicken decal on the front hood. Even from this distance, I could tell that Carlos, as always, was sitting in the front seat.

He'd begun these lonely vigils about a year ago.

Carlos had once said, uncharacteristically, "I can find anything," and he'd apparently found out the truth about Vincente, although he'd never said a word. He never gave the slightest indication. He just sat there in the parking lot on Sunday afternoons, as if supporting me somehow, as if somehow understanding what I was going through, and I wondered, as I did each and every week, if Carlos knew that I knew that he knew.

William Baer worked briefly in New York City's fashion district after high school. He's now the award-winning author of twenty-five books, including the first three novels in the popular *New Jersey Noir* mystery series. He's a graduate of NYU, Rutgers, South Carolina, Johns Hopkins, and USC's School of Cinema, where he received the Jack Nicholson Screenwriting Award. He's also been the recipient of a Fulbright, a Guggenheim, and a Creative Writing Fellowship in fiction from the National Endowment for the Arts.

FROM MANY WORDS PRESS

Novels by William Baer:
> *Murder in Times Square: A Deirdre Novel, Book One*
> *Advocatus Diaboli: A Catholic Novel*

Forthcoming:
> *Murder in Nashville: A Deirdre Novel, Book Two*
> *Novel: A Novel*
> *Jacinta: A Catholic Novel*
> *Annie Oakley Mystery: A Novel*
> *Central Park: A Novel*
> *The Heretic: A Catholic Novel*
> *Screenplay: A Novel*
> *The Sweet Science: A Novel*
> *The Gravedigger: A Novel*
> *Crossbow: A Novel*
> *Equinox: A Novel*

FROM ABLE MUSE PRESS

Novels by William Baer:
> *New Jersey Noir: A Jack Colt Novel, Book One*
> *New Jersey Noir: Cape May: A Jack Colt Novel, Book Two*
> *New Jersey Noir: Barnegat Light: A Jack Colt Novel, Book Three*

www.manywords.com

www.ablemusepress.com